Human Matter

T0087727

Latin American Literature in Translation Series

Other Books in the Series:
The Enlightened Army by David Toscana (2018)

Human Matter
A Fiction

Rodrigo Rey Rosa

Translated by Eduardo Aparicio

University of Texas Press ♥ Austin

© 2009, 2017 by Rodrigo Rey Rosa
English translation copyright © 2019 by the University of Texas Press
All rights reserved
Printed in the United States of America

Project editor: Lynne Chapman
Cover design: Isaac Tobin
Interior typesetting: Cassandra Cisneros
Typeset in Adobe Garamond Pro
Book cover printed by Phoenix Color, interior by Sheridan Books

Requests for permission to reproduce material from this work should be sent to:
    Permissions
    University of Texas Press
    P.O. Box 7819
    Austin, TX 78713-7819
    utpress.utexas.edu/rp-form

∞ The paper used in this book meets the minimum requirements of ANSI/NISO
Z39.48-1992 (R1997) (Permanence of Paper).

Library of Congress Cataloging-in-Publication Data

Names: Rey Rosa, Rodrigo, 1958–, author. | Aparicio, Eduardo, translator.
Title: Human matter / Rodrigo Rey Rosa ; translated by Eduardo Aparicio.
Other titles: El material humano. English
Description: Austin : University of Texas Press, 2019. | Series: Latin American
    Literature in Translation series
Identifiers: LCCN 2018034576
    ISBN 978-1-4773-1646-7 (pbk. : alk. paper)
    ISBN 978-1-4773-1864-5 (library e-book)
    ISBN 978-1-4773-1865-2 (nonlibrary e-book)
Subjects: LCSH: Guatemala—History—Fiction.
Classification: LCC PQ7499.2.R38 M3813 2019 | DDC 863/.64—dc23
LC record available at https://lccn.loc.gov/2018034576

doi:10.7560/316467

For Marta García Salas

Though it may not seem to be,
though it may not want to seem to be,
this is a work of fiction.

Contents

Human Matter

Introduction

Shortly before I became aware of the existence of the famous Archive that I've been wanting to work on, in the very early hours of June 17, 2005, a fire and a series of explosions partially destroyed an ammunition depot belonging to the National Army outside of Guatemala City, where approximately one ton of missiles of various calibers was stored, part of the supplies left over from the domestic war that began in 1960 and ended in 1996. An official from the Human Rights Ombudsman's Office was assigned to investigate the existence of other ammunition depots that could pose a similar danger. He visited the facilities at La Isla, in the northernmost end of the city, a complex of police buildings that includes the Police Academy, a criminal investigation center, a vast dump of wrecked vehicles, the police canine unit, an abandoned hospital, and the ammunition depot. Mysteriously, the explosive devices (sticks of dynamite, grenades, mortars) that were supposed to be stored there had disappeared the day before the investigation. However, in an adjacent building, which had perhaps operated as a hospital but which according to the investigators at the Ombudsman's Office was used as a torture center (the windows in almost every room had been sealed with bricks or cinder blocks), the investigator from the Ombudsman's Office discovered a room full of papers, files, boxes, and bags of police documents. This was true of almost all the rooms and halls on the first and second floors of this building and other adjacent structures.

When the National Police was dismantled following the

peace accords signed in 1996, someone ordered the transfer to this site of the Archive from the former National Police headquarters and from other regional police stations, and the eighty million–plus documents presently housed at the Archive—including record books dating from the 1890s—had stayed hidden since then, until July 6, 2005, when the local press reported the unlikely and fortunate discovery.

When I first interviewed the head of the Archive Recovery Project, my intent was to find out about cases of intellectuals and artists who were the subject of police investigation—or who had collaborated with the police as informers or accusers—in the twentieth century. But in view of the chaotic state of the material ("It will take about fifteen years to classify the documents," the chief told me), that idea had to be discarded as impracticable. However, he himself invited me to visit the Archive and mentioned a department that might be of special interest, the Identification Bureau, which had been preserved, almost miraculously—if not in its entirety, at least in good part, and all in one place. In addition, the documents it contained covered a wide span of time and had already been cataloged in their entirety.

For several weeks after the Archive was found, no one had noticed the existence of the cards and files that had belonged to this Bureau. Between two buildings of the former hospital complex, there was a mound of earth marked by the trail made by the wheelbarrows that would come and go, loaded with documents that were being relocated for cleaning, cataloging, and digitizing. Shortly after the rainy season, with the onset of the drought, the surface of the mound, where the grass had already been growing, cracked slightly, and someone saw that underneath the soil there were papers, cards, photographs. The traffic of wheelbarrows was immediately stopped, and the papers were examined. They turned out to be the police identity files and other documents that make up the vestiges of the Bureau. If I was interested in seeing this—the chief told me—he would authorize me to enter the Archive, and perhaps, he added, after seeing the Bureau I could visit other sections. For my own safety, and because some of the cases opened after 1970 could still be active or pending in court, he asked me not to consult any documents dated after that year.

On the day of my first visit to the Archive I met Ariadna Sandoval, a twenty-three-year-old archivist. Her job was to clean and catalog the documents belonging to the Identification Bureau.

"At the foot of the records originating from the different police bodies and received at the Bureau, there is a name that will appear constantly: Benedicto Tun. He founded the Bureau himself, in 1922, and worked there classifying and analyzing files until 1970, when he retired. He was the only Bureau chief all those years. Maybe this could serve as a connecting thread for your . . . *research*?" Ariadna said to me as she showed me the boxes where she had been storing the recovered files for almost a year.

I began to frequent the Archive as a kind of entertainment, and as I usually do when I have nothing to write, nothing really to say, during those days I filled a series of notebooks, sketchbooks, and loose sheets with simple impressions and observations. Every morning for almost three months I traveled from the southernmost to the northernmost end of Guatemala City to visit the Archive. I suppose those who were employed there—both the humanities majors and the former rebels-turned-archivists involved in the cleaning and cataloging of the documents, as well as the police officers

3

who watched over them—saw me as a tourist or an inconvenient and opportunistic latecomer. For my part, beyond the information I had hoped to obtain in that maze of millions of police records accumulated for more than a century and preserved by chance, the circumstances and the atmosphere at the Archive in La Isla, after that initial visit, had started to seem like something out of a novel, or perhaps something that could even be turned into a novel, a kind of *micro-chaos*, the telling of which could serve as a coda for the singular danse macabre of our last century.

First Notebook: Modo & Modo

Thursday, December 14, 9 a.m. At the Archive.

I decide to make a list of the most striking or grotesque records. I suppose that this task, as Ariadna suggested, would have a kind of Kafkaesque quality to it, and could provide a glimpse into a man, clerk Benedicto Tun, with no college degree, whose long and peculiar criminological trajectory in a country with a political history as turbulent as Guatemala is something of a feat.

The record cards originally used by Tun employed the Vucetich system, which could include, in addition to the name and fingerprints of the persons involved, the reason for initiating a record on them, their place of residence, marital status, profession and background, and any special observations. This system underwent some modifications in 1931 (such as the introduction of cards to replace strips of paper), and in 1969 the Henry system was imposed by the US Embassy—so that American investigators could interpret the records without difficulty. In that system only a person's name, age, and fingerprints are recorded. In addition, beginning in 1971, all men in Guatemala, upon reaching adulthood and requesting their national identity card, became a part of a database housed at the Identification Bureau, which the government of Guatemala shared with the US government, according to a document preserved in the Identification Bureau. Both systems designate a place for the photograph of the accused, and more than a few of these photos have been preserved.

The records are on yellowed 4" × 6" cards, which have

now been nibbled away by humidity and the passage of time. At the bottom of almost all the ones that I have reviewed is the seal and signature of Benedicto Tun.

Second Notebook: Black Binding

Fate is always excessive: it punishes a moment of distraction, the random act of making a left instead of a right, sometimes with death.

Borges, quoted by Bioy Casares

Archive. Thursday afternoon.

I. POLITICAL CRIMES

- Aguilar Elías, León, born in 1921. Black, slim, straight black hair, half of right big toe missing. Booked in 1948 for criticizing the Supreme Government of the Revolution, in 1955 for allegedly claiming communist sympathies.

- Aguirre Cook, Natsuel, born in 1925. Office clerk, married. Booked in July 1954 for being a communist. (On the verso and attached sheet): Charged as one the most dangerous communist leaders, right-hand man to Carlos Manuel Pellicer. Agitator in the rural areas of Chicacao and Suchitepéquez, and accomplice in the death of the local mayor. He later operated a clandestine radio station out of the San Julián estate in Tiquisate. Under the administration of Dr. Juan José Arévalo, he was employed in the Ministry of Foreign Affairs. Detained when requesting a driver's license.

- Ávila Aroche, Jesús, born in 1931. Black. (1.86 m.) Marimba player. Single. Lives with his mother. Booked for shining shoes without a license. Charged with larceny in March 1962. With theft in December 1962. With kidnapping in 1963.

- Aguilar García, Benito. Born in 1923 in Escuintla. Single. Lives with mother and brothers. Booked in 1948 when seeking to enlist with the Civil Guard. Discharged and transferred to the National Committee Against Communism in 1955 for being part of the Civil Guard platoon that was sent to Puerto Barrios as a punitive

11

expedition under the command of Lieutenant Cornelio Lone Mejía in June of 1954 to carry out acts of genocide (*in the last days of the Revolutionary Government*).

- Barrientos, Luis Alfredo. Born in 1924. Journalist. Booked in 1956 for demonstrating. In 1958 for spreading outlandish ideas.

- Chávez Zacarías, Horacio. Born in 1930. Booked for being an agitator at El Porvenir farm.

- Cao Chub, Sebastián. Born (date unknown). Lives with his concubine Isidra Caal. Laborer. Illiterate. Booked in 1957 for causing a fire on Ricardo Kreb's property.

- Cotón, Ramírez. Born in 1927 in Malacatán, San Marcos. Booked for being a liaison between communist nationals and exiles in Mexico.

- Cabrera García, Leopoldo. Born in 1931. Classical musician. Booked without a motive in 1956.

- Cante Villagrán, Balvino. Born in 1930. Tiler. Booked in 1950 for no reason.

- Castillo Román, Jorge. Born in 1920. Chauffeur. Booked in 1955 for being a communist.

- Chacón Lara, Miguel. Born in 1926. Tinsmith (in Antigua). Booked in 1943 for insubordination.

- Coronado Coro, Álvaro. Born in 1940. Telegraph operator. Booked in 1962 for sabotage.

- Díaz Paredes, Fausto. Born in 1945. Tractor driver. Booked in 1970 for attacks against democratic institutions and possession of war supplies. For robbery, plagiarism, and murder in 1972.

- Figueroa Estrada, Rafael. Born in 1924 in the capital. Farmer. Booked in 1955 for being a terrorist.

- Figueroa Vides, Rodolfo. Born in 1930. Journalist. Married. Booked for no reason in 1956.

- Fajardo Pérez, Antonio. Born in 1937. Student, lives with his mother. Booked in 1956 for sedition and rebellion.

- García Soto, Gonzalo. Born in 1930. Bricklayer's helper. Booked in 1960 for violating curfew.

- García, Domínguez. Born in 1927. Driver. Booked in 1964 for possession of explosives.

- Gallardo Ordóñez, Mario. Born in 1929. Leatherworker. Booked in 1959 for distributing subversive propaganda.

- Galvez Sandoval, María Virginia. Born in 1932. Teacher without a degree. Booked in 1954 for being affiliated with the Party for Revolutionary Action.

- Gudiel López, María Luisa. Born in 1934. Lives with her parents. Booked in 1956 for weapons possession.

- Hernández Carrillo, Víctor. Born in 1910 in Puerto Barrios. Fisherman. Booked in 1963 for theft of telephone cable.

- Ingenieros Fernández, Pablo. Born in 1950. Auto body repair worker. Booked for desecrating the national flag.

- Lorenzana Marcio, Iván. Born in 1935. Lives with mother and brothers in Zone 1. Draftsman. Booked in 1960 for possession of war supplies.

- Molina López, Efraín. Born in 1932. Typographer. Booked in 1960 for allegedly being responsible for a bomb explosion.

- Méndez Arriaza, Pedro. Born in 1925. Dental technician. Booked in 1961 for subversive activities.

- Nadal Chinchilla, Manuel de Jesús. Born in 1930. Single. Classical musician. Booked in 1955 for being a communist sympathizer.

- Ochoa Santizo, Jorge. Born in 1943. Auto body repair worker. Booked in 1960 for suspicious activity. Lives with his mother, a whore.

Friday.

II. COMMON CRIMES

- Velásquez Vásquez, Salvador. Born in 1925. Shoeshine. Booked in 1937 for participating in forbidden games. In 1940 for theft. Set free in 1941.

- Menchú Flavian, Juan. Born in 1924. Merchant. Booked in 1940. Peddler without a license.

- Papandreas Kaleb, Jorge. Born in 1927. Student. Booked in 1942 for disobeying his father. In 1965 for fraud and death threats.

- Rosales Vidal, Francisco. Born in 1925. Typographer. Booked in 1940 for playing soccer on public streets.

- Figueroa García, Florentino. Born in 1925. Shoeshine. Lives alone. Booked in 1945 (*Revolutionary Government*) for shining shoes without a license.

- Castañeda Contreras, Catalina. Born in 1926. Domestic worker. Booked in 1940 for practicing clandestine prostitution at home and in La Selecta restaurant.

- Mejía de Mendizábal, Julia. Born in 1920. Home address Aurora Alley, #11. Booked in 1940 for attempted murder of her husband, Gabriel Mendizábal.

- Masserli R., Carlos Fernando. Born in 1926. Lives with his parents. Apprentice mechanic. Booked in 1941 for disobeying his father. In 1948 for pederasty.

- Chávez A., Luis. Born in 1921. Lives with his family. Booked in 1940 for vagrancy. In 1954 for theft.

- Herrera Hernández, Petrona. Born in 1925. Lives alone. Domestic worker. Booked in 1941 for stealing a poncho, a sheet, a dress, and a mat from Mr. Justo Espada España.

- Sarceño O., Juan. Born in 1925. Gardener. Lives with his sister. Booked in 1945 (*Revolutionary Government*) for dancing the tango in the brewery "El Gaucho," where it is prohibited.

- Funes Coronado, Víctor. Born in 1923 in Champerico. Single. Booked in 1942 for fishing with a cast net during closed season.

- Marroquín Cardona, Vicente. Born in 1926. No profession. Booked in 1939 for complicity in bicycle theft.

- Chávez Coronado, María. Born in 1924 (a minor). Profession: sex worker. She has neither children nor a known male partner. Illiterate. Arrested in August 1939 in Barberena for performing lewd acts in public.

- Pineda C., Marta. Born in 1914. No permanent address. Booked in 1945 for exercising clandestine free love. Additional information: unbearable and insulting woman. She lives alone.

- Carranza Ávila, Rosa María. Born in 1920. Domestic worker. Booked in 1944 for committing adultery in her home.

- García Aceituno, Francisca. Born in 1925. Profession: sex worker. Booked in 1940 for selling sweets without a license.

- Santos Aguilar, Perfecta. Born in 1922. Booked in 1943 for having a venereal disease.

- Robles M., Ana Lucrecia. Born in 1932. Without a trade. Booked in 1944 for peddling milk without a license.

- Aceytuno Salvador, Luis Fabio. Born in 1920 in Santa Cruz, El Quiché. Booked in 1939 for cohabiting with a sow.

- Castillo, Bartolo. Born in 1899. Carpenter. Booked in 1933. Accused by Laureano E. Girón of killing a man a long time ago, and for fraud amounting to $14,000 when he was mayor of Azacualpa.

- Echevarría C., Dionisio Mauricio. Born in 1930. Booked in 1958 for complicity in theft of chickens.

- Cabrera, David (son of Rómulo Zamora and Socorro Zamora). Born in 1925. No profession. Booked in 1934 for begging.

- Vásquez V., Mariano. Born in 1923. Farmer. Booked in 1935 for loitering on street corners and for vagrancy.

- Charnaud, José Luis. Born in 1910. Student. Booked in 1935 for document forgery.

- Rabanales Morales, Mario. Born in 1920. Printer. Booked

in 1944 for loitering on street corners and for mocking the motherland.

- Mejía Melgar, José. Born in 1920. Shoemaker. Booked in 1945 for pickpocketing at the town festival in Pasaco.

- Espinoza G., Silvia. Born in 1918. Booked in 1936 for assault, scratches and blows to Dolores Aceituno.

- Castillo F., Ricardo. Born in 1914. Florist. Booked in 1941 for recidivist loitering.

- Carrillo Soto, Encarnación. Born in 1921. Farm worker. Booked in 1944 for assault and for being an alleged rustler.

- Quiroa G., Ramiro. Born in 1929 in Escuintla. Office worker.

- Nils Martínez, Otto. Born in 1937. Typographer. Booked in 1952 for vagrancy and for frequenting brothels while underage.

- Galindo Méndez, Francisco. Born in 1915 in Tecpán. Painter. Booked in 1937 for vagrancy and for being incorrigible. In 1938 for disorderly conduct while drunk. In 1944 for abandonment of home (being the father of two children).

- Serrano E., Vicente. Born in 1926. Booked in 1937 for shining boots without a license.

- Lemus J., Carlos. Born in 1920. No profession. Booked in 1938 for theft. In 1942 for illegal gambling. In 1959 for possession of drugs. In 1961 for attempted fraud.

- García Castro, Ángela. Born in 1924. Booked in 1938 for witchcraft practices in house #12, Avenida de la Industria, Zone 9.

- Reyes Campos, Dolores. Born in 1920. Domestic worker. Single. Booked for practicing witchcraft.

- Izil Yaguas, José Juan. Born in (date unknown). Lives alone and has no fixed address. Booked in 1938 for not wearing an apron while selling bread.

- Aguliar C., Pedro. Born in 1922. Booked in 1938 for attempted rape of Bernarda Reyes, twelve years old. In 1946 for theft.

- Caal Mocú, Julia. Born in 1921 in Cobán. Domestic worker. Lives with her mom. Booked in 1939 for harming trees on public walks.

- Petronilo, Moreira. (Black, round face.) Born in 1923 in Lívingston. Laborer. Booked in 1939 for mob fighting.

- Navarro G., Ignacio. Born in (does not know the date). Acrobat. Widower. Booked in 1939 for assaulting Mr. Francisco García.

- Ortega B., Enrique. He was born in 1921 in Mazatenango. Farm owner. Booked in 1950 for whipping his wife.

- Larios M., Manuel. Born in 1921 in Sololá. Day laborer. Booked in 1939 for contraband of alcohol. Clay implements were confiscated from him.

- Ucelo H., Lorenzo. Born in 1921 in San José Pinula. Farm laborer. Booked in 1938 for having set fire to a mountain.

- García G., Paulino. Born in 1920. Waiter. Booked in 1938 for insubordination against Andrés Caicedo, his boss.

- Cáceres, Diega de. (Black race.) Born in (does not know the date) in Lívingston. Midwife. Booked for practicing without a license.

- Us Castro, Gregorio. Born in (does not know the date). Day laborer. Single. Attention: He is in a conjugal relationship with Juana Quintanilla, has three children and a brother who is mute. Booked in 1938 for being a dishonest worker at the Milan estate.

- Godoy O., Mario. Born in 1920. Student. Arrested for impertinence.

- Ramírez y Ramírez, Anacleto. Born in 1920 in Jutiapa. Day laborer. Single. Booked for stealing twenty-five quetzals from Jesús Álvarez.

- Ochaeta F., Armando. Born in 1921 in Flores, Petén. Tailor. Booked at the request of his brother Genaro Ochaeta, for threatening him with a penknife.

- Ortiz V., René. Born in 1922. Student. Booked in 1947 for shooting with a blowpipe in the Lux movie theater.

- Valdés P., Sergio Estuardo. Born in 1931. Photographer. Booked in 1952 for releasing a vulture in the Capitol movie theater.

- Mazariegos Piedrasanta, Gerardo. Born in 1920 in Xela. Classical musician. Detained in 1939 in Retalhuleu for illegal gambling.

- Pérez Gonzáles, Pedro. Born in (does not know the date) in Retalhuleu. Detained in 1940 in San Marcos for complicity in the contraband of opium.

- Pérez Gómez, Alejandro. Born in 1923 in Antigua. Day laborer. Booked for carrying a rubber sling, a club, and a penknife. He has no ID. Lives alone.

- Monzón López, José. Born in 1921. Day laborer. Arrested for not carrying any kind of a municipal tax receipt or his employment log.

- Méndez V., Raúl. Born in 1929. Student (minor). Booked in 1940 at the request of his grandmother, for misbehavior. In 1945 for drunk and disorderly conduct. In 1950 for rape. In 1955 for requesting admission into the Civil Guard.

- Vizcaíno Rojas, Rodolfo. Born in 1921 in Guatemala City. Student. Booked in 1943 for theft and for slapping his mother.

- Mendoza M., Dolores. Born in 1927 in Tiquisate. Domestic worker. Resides in the Hospital of Tiquisate. Booked for immoral acts at a public dance.

- Ramírez M., Eusebia. Born in 1925 in Escuintla. Signed in 1942 for practicing free love.

- Brown, Alfredo. Black race. Born (does not know the date) in New York, USA. Sailor. He does not speak Spanish. Booked in 1939 for quarreling with Marcus Müller.

- Flores, Rolando. Mulatto. Born in (does not know the date). Day laborer. Resides at Petén farm, in Tiquisate. Arrested for defamation. He claimed to have had intercourse with Carmen Morales, who at the request of her mother underwent medical examination, confirming her virginity.

- Figueroa Santiago, Boluciano. Born in 1927. Tailor. Booked in 1955 for challenging someone to a duel.

- Gálvez Ravanales, María. Born in (does not know the date). Domestic worker. Single. Booked in 1956 for marijuana trafficking.

- Zamora del Valle, Salvador. Born in 1929. Shoemaker. Booked in 1963 for marijuana trafficking.

- Barreondo Flores, Tomás. Born in 1927 in Guatemala City. Student (minor). Booked in 1937 for marijuana trafficking.

- Urrutia R., Jorge. Born in 1935 in Guatemala City. Classical musician. Booked in 1956 for promoting the use of illegal drugs.

- Arrivillaga P., Delfino Bernardino. Born in 1927. Day laborer in San Martín Jilotepeque. Booked in 1955 for practicing sorcery.

- Barrientos Ortiz, Jorge. Born in 1926 in Guatemala City. Baker. Single. Booked in 1955 for practicing sorcery.

- Ninassi Tacchi, Giuseppe. Italian. Booked in 1955 for being a member of a band of counterfeiters who forged bank notes and checks, captured in the Republic of Honduras in September of 1955.

- Tacaús López, Máximo. Born in 1928. Weaver. Lives alone in Totonicapán. Booked in 1953 because he consumes liquor with other individuals who specialize in undressing drunken night owls.

- Marroquín P., Santiago. Born in 1923 in Santa Catarina Pinula. Farmer. Booked in 1953 for growing marijuana.

- Reyes V., Dionisia. Born in 1931 in El Progreso. Booked for the homicide of her younger brother, Januario Reyes, with a shotgun.

- Guillermo Elezcano, Lorenzo. Spaniard. Born in 1931. Farmer in the Matamoros Valley. Single. Booked in 1960 before being expelled from the country as undesirable.

- Mejía Paz, José Gaspar. Born in 1933 in Totonicapán. Farmer. Booked in 1950 for killing Mr. Antonio Sac Mon, with a stick.

Attention: He has a thirty-year-old brother whose name is also Gaspar and who is also in prison.

- Chacón F., Gumercinda. Born in 1930 in the capital city. Domestic worker. Single. Booked for practicing occult sciences.

- Ballesteros Noya, Pancracio. Born in 1927 in Alajuela, Costa Rica. Tailor and artist. Lives with Virginia Castellanos. Has two children. Booked in 1958 for exercising palmistry and fortune-telling, swindling the public. He also exploits ladies of the night.

- Marroquín Alvizures, Marco Antonio. Born in 1933. Office clerk. Booked for publishing obscenities.

- Carrillo Martínez, Jorge Mario. Born in 1929. Accountant. Booked in 1948 for serious insults and for damaging the blossoms of the flowerbed at the National Palace.

- Flores R., Simón. Born in 1952. Couturier. Booked in 1960 for recidivist streetwalking.

- Carrera Mazariegos, Gilberto. Born in 1920. Hatter. Married, with five children. Booked in 1941 for rape.

- Cervantes M., Procopio. (Strong build.) Born in 1928 in Zacapa. Day laborer. Booked in 1951 for the homicide of J. Paulo Pérez, with a hoe.

- Chacón V., Rafael. Born in 1926. Traveling agent. Married. Booked in 1967 for rape and fraud.

- Perdomo O., José. Born in 1934. No job. Booked in 1958 for theft of an old hammer. In 1964 for violation of the health code.

- Antunes Pérez, Emilia. Born in 1920. Domestic worker in

the capital city. Lives with her children. Booked in 1955 for prostitution.

• Novales, Dolores. Born in 1919. Honduran (Puerto Cortez). Booked in 1955 because she wants to leave prostitution and lead an honest life.

Afternoon.

III. POSTMORTEM FILES

† Ruano Coronado, María Consuelo. Born in 1918. Booked in 1937 for marijuana trafficking and possession. Shot dead in 1980.

† XX. Traits: Between thirty-two and thirty-seven years old. Working class look (tailor, merchant, or driver). Dark complexion. Strangled in the street in 1980.

† XX. Traits: Twenty-plus years old. Straight black hair. Concave nose. Shot dead in front of Doresley department store in 1980.

† Zamora Enamorado, José Cecilio. Living in Puerto Barrios. Day laborer. Details: right index finger amputated. Detained November 4, 1961, for contraband. Killed with a sharp object in 1973.

† XX. Hands and feet tied with banana rope, beaten, and thrown into the river. Clarification: When proceeding to fingerprint the aforementioned corpse, I ran into the difficulty that the fingers were shriveled, making it difficult to take rolled impressions, and although I also attempted the injection technique, that too was unsuccessful. I had no choice but to cut off those fingers that I considered best for the purpose. Signature: José Héctor Terraza T., December 7, 1974.

Note: In an envelope attached to this file I found a strip of paper with the printed grid to set the fingerprints. But, instead of the typical ink spots, there were a few pieces of tissue that resembled dried rose petals. Upon closer examination, they turned out to be human skin.

Other professions registered in the files of the Bureau:

Coal merchant
Typist
Drill operator
Plumber
Train brakeman
Stonecutter
Weaver
Mechanic
Travel agent
Railroad worker
Sawyer
Truck assistant

It would not be wise to conclude anything on the basis of the chaotic and capricious information contained in a series of police files that resisted time and weathering by chance. The number of files that were lost or that disintegrated into humus is certainly considerable. But the list shows the arbitrary and often perverse nature of our own unique justice system, which laid the foundations for the widespread violence that was unleashed on the country in the eighties and whose aftermath we are still living. (It helps to remember that misdemeanors, like not carrying the "employment log" that was required of indigenous people dispossessed of their lands by government decree, continued to be penalized in 1944 with forced labor in government works and on private farms—the very farms created with the spoils of the "Indian territories.") Our own unique system? Back in the eighteenth century, commenting on the treatise *On Crimes and Punishments* by Cesare Beccaria, Voltaire wrote: "It seems that in times of feudal anarchy, the princes and the lords, being quite poor, tried to increase their treasures by stripping and condemning their vassals, thus creating a revenue stream from their very crime."

More Voltaire:

The weaknesses brought to light please only malice, unless they instruct by the misfortunes that have followed them or because of the virtues that have repaired them.

What can we think of these errors and many others? Will we just content ourselves with moaning about human nature? There were cases when it was necessary to avenge it.

Not everyone is allowed to commit the same misdeeds.

First Sketchbook: Green Cover with Indian Motifs

Monday, December 18. Midday break at the Archives.

Smell of pork rinds. In a room with windows that overlook a hallway, where I look at identification cards, I overhear an archivist, sensing the smell, telling a colleague:

"It smells of roasted pig, did they kill your husband?" Although some of the girls seem very attractive to me, for the moment I would not be willing to leave my circles, so to speak, for one of them. I think that the opposite is true for L.A. and her ex-partner (or was he a gold digger?).

A little bored, a little frightened. Upset (although also much amused) by some passages in *Borges* by Bioy that I read during the breaks. On the other hand, resentment toward B+, who has proposed another break. I still miss her. However, when I think about her, I say to myself: "Better that way."

Tuesday at noon.

They just took me out of the old hospital room, a cool room, although a little damp, where I was working. They have hired a handful of additional archivists to accelerate the cataloging process, and they are now moving work tables around to settle them in. They move me to one of the new wards, with a low roof of sheet metal, where it is very hot. If I did not come here on my own initiative, I would consider complaining. I have the impression that it's some kind of punishment. There's no one else in this ward, I suppose because of the heat. Wearing the required latex gloves, my hands sweat profusely. The "canine unit," which houses about fifty dogs of different breeds, is directly next to me, and the constant and sometimes furious barking is not conducive to concentration. Beyond the kennels, in a vacant lot, there are piles of car wrecks. During one of the breaks (while archivists and police officers play a friendly game of football), I examine the remains of cars that have accumulated over half a century. A Renault split in half catches my eye, as does the fuselage of a Cessna plane, which I suppose crashed somewhere within the city limits. The wind kicks up a small swirl of cream-colored dust.

A burglar alarm goes off somewhere.

Wednesday.

Luis Galíndez, one of the archivists, a few years older than me—a man with a tired look and straight gray hair, with whom I have established a degree of friendship—approaches at break time to give me, surreptitiously, a manila envelope that, he tells me, contains a long list prepared by the Guatemalan Military Police in the eighties and nineties. It contains photos, information, and personal data of individuals who had disappeared (or would disappear) for political reasons. The list, from a secret military file, was "leaked" about a year ago, and although today it is freely accessible (it can be read on a website), Galíndez asks me not to say how I got it. Then he says that next month they will give the workers at the Archive a course on "Violence, Power, and Politics" in Ciudad Vieja. Apparently, if I wish, I can attend. I make the necessary arrangements and register.

Monday. Eight in the morning. Ciudad Vieja.

Dr. Gustavo Novales, who teaches the course, begins by explaining why he decided to study the "sociology of violence." In the seventies, he had a close call, almost getting kidnapped and tortured because of his "subversive activities." On that occasion, his parents were captured and tortured to death, just like a neighbor of theirs, who vaguely looked like Dr. Novales, with whom they confused him. Exiled to Mexico, he began studying this subject—he tells us—to "draw some benefit from his experiences as a victim of state violence," and to find a rationale for the things that happened to him and his family.

Dr. Novales dresses elegantly in an English style (a short coat, a tweed jacket under it, a sober tie) and presents his points clearly and in a mild-mannered way, but at certain times one can see in his eyes a glow of tamed dogmatism. He divides state terrorism into two categories: state terrorism properly speaking, and revolutionary violence, which is its corollary. Regarding the general causes of violence, he says that it has been a constant "since the dawn of humanity"—take, for example, the struggle of *Homo sapiens* versus the Neanderthal, which ended with the defeat of Neanderthal man and his extinction.

"Only human beings can be violent. The predatory behavior of animals does not imply violence," he says.

He delivers the following axioms:

—Every act of violence is an act of power.

—Not every act of power is an act of violence.

—Violence implies the use of physical force.

—Force is not necessary in all cases; the threat alone may suffice, such as the white handprints on the homes of alleged communists in Guatemala in the sixties and seventies.*

—A weak state needs to exercise terror.

* Mano Blanca (White Hand) was the name of an organization linked to the army and dedicated to the extermination of communists and their sympathizers.

Afternoon.

Among the examples of violence as an act of resistance, the doctor mentions:

A riot: An act of collective violence (which can end in lynching) against the embodiment of power or the nearest authority. "This movement is spontaneous, emotional, not premeditated, caused by a feeling of grievance transformed into anger."

An uprising: It is not ephemeral or spontaneous. It can generate a "revolutionary situation" (that is, one where "those below" can no longer tolerate their living conditions and dominant groups can no longer govern).

A revolution: A generalized uprising that leads to a displacement of power in a nation or in critical geographical areas.

He clarifies that the concept of revolution is ever changing. Today, revolutions tend to be neither violent nor abrupt. Examples: those of Venezuela, Bolivia, and Ecuador.

Tuesday. Eight in the morning.

Cases:

Brazilian dictatorship: 185 disappeared by state terror in twenty years.

Argentine dictatorship: 30,000 disappeared in ten years.

Guatemalan dictatorship: 45,000 missing (and 150,000 executions) in thirty-six years.

The Guatemalan army—according to some reports like REMHI* and the CEH†—was responsible for about 95 percent of deaths and forced disappearances, while the guerrillas, for less than 5 percent.

----

* *Recovery of Historical Memory*, conducted by the Catholic Church.

† *Commission for Historical Clarification*, at the request of the United Nations.

After 1966, the authorities in Guatemala do not report any more political prisoners; then begins the period of forced disappearances, clandestine prisons, and extrajudicial executions.

Belatedly, political prisoners were granted typewriters to "render reports" (denunciations). Possibilities: invention and buying time.

Measures imposed by the insurgency on its members in case of capture:

—Resist for a prudent amount of time to allow for dismantling of structures (then restructure them differently).

—Do not reestablish contact with any members in case of escape or liberation, under threat of death.

The doctor cites the well-known case of two young guerrilla women who were captured and then used as "sex servants" by state agents for several months. After a somewhat doubtful "escape," they went into exile in Nicaragua, where they reestablished contact with former guerrilla comrades. They were tried for treason ("from within the subversive ranks"), found guilty, and executed.

Afternoon.

Ricardo Ramírez and the 1967 "March Document," in which the decision is made to change the "combat scenario," and on which is based an attempt to involve the Mayan population—previously excluded—in the armed struggle. "The action must be localized away from government influence and close to the Indian communities." The previous strategy, which had failed, was one focused on urban guerillas, with other centers of guerilla activity in uninhabited areas or areas inhabited by "non-indigenous" people.

Wednesday. Eight in the morning.

During a question-and-answer session, I make the mistake of asking the following:

Given the fact that the Mayan people are the base of the Guatemalan social pyramid, a revolutionary struggle in their favor could be justified; but as the majority of the Mayan peasants are illiterate, it can be assumed that they did not share the Marxist ideology of the revolutionary leaders. At the time of this decision to change the "combat scenario"—following the Vietnamese experience and knowing the new counterinsurgency strategy of "taking the water away from the fish"—it was natural to think about the possible risk of a government reaction that would determine the extermination of broad sectors of the Indian population. Was this—the fact of endangering that particular sector of the population with extermination—a subject of debate?

The answer is no, this had not been the subject of debate. After delivering the answer with disgust, Dr. Novales characterizes my question as "extremely unfriendly." Another of the course attendees adds that my question seemed paternalistic, that he had known some Mayan people who did want to fight.

Afternoon.

I do not know if it is as an indirect retaliation that the doctor then speaks in a tone of confidence of a "bourgeois friend" who, in the late seventies, resigned from the board of directors of a family business "because in one of the meetings, they proposed the murder of a union leader." I think I know who that is. I can think of three friends of mine (one of them disappeared) who were members of boards of directors at powerful companies, and who, because of their leftist tendencies, became involved in a revolutionary movement and ended up in exile for some years. Two things occur to me. First: although it is likely—as has been proven in more than one case—that some of the directors of large companies felt threatened by the trade union movement at the time and planned and carried out the murders of trade unionists, it's hard to believe that they would have discussed these murders in a general session. Second: if it is the friend whom I think it is, it seems reasonable to me that she would resign from the board of directors, but should she not also have relinquished all stock in a company that was clearly criminal? Should she not at least have opted to sell those shares? As far as I know, she did not.

Thursday, January 18. B+'s birthday.

Today I resume note taking after several days of apathy.

I have finished reviewing the files of the Identification Bureau. I ask to see lists of official executions, whistleblowers. . . . For some reason, I cannot have access to those documents "yet." They move me back to the hospital, to a room on the second floor, where half a dozen archivists are dusting off meeting minutes and other documents before they are digitized. While they are working, they listen to boleros.

This (Area 2, Room 2, Section 3, Wall B) is the old Police Library. I take a look. I ask to see three or four volumes of the collection of Yearly Reports from the National Police, titled *Memorias de Labores de la Policía Nacional.*

Sandra Gil, an older archivist who resembles a stern teacher, has just handed me the volumes. She chews gum, loudly. A female colleague comments without addressing anyone in particular:

"There are those of us who think, and those who chew gum."

The other responds:

"Oh, Lord, illuminate them, or eliminate them."

From the Yearly Report, 1938, Chapter XXVI: "It has been said that our body is actually a given amount of compressed air that lives in the air. Could it not be said that the soul is an embodied fragment of society that lives in society? . . . A criminal would then be a social microbe."—Professor G. Tarde, criminologist.

In Chapter XXXI, I find a "Report from the Identification Bureau," headed by clerk Benedict Tun, "whose participation in the investigation of criminal acts has been invaluable in the most important inquiries carried out by the Police . . ."

Afternoon.

Lunch with B+ in a trendy restaurant. Mediocre food. Then, in my apartment, prolonged lovemaking session, extraordinarily intense and pleasant—at least for me.

Is it possible to know whether it was the same for both of us? I do not think so.

Very brief nap.

I keep leafing through the Yearly Reports, while I wait to be allowed to see more interesting documents.

Personal characteristics of criminals apprehended in 1943:

Between 21 and 30 years old: 36%
Single: 81%
Males: 82%
Workers: 28%
Mestizo: 11%

Suicides:

Between 21 and 30 years old: 36%
Single: 70%
Workers: 23%
Mestizo: 96%

I find an entry in Google under the name of Tun. According to an article titled "The Smell of Blood," by Alfredo Sagastume, Benedicto Tun was also a "bloodhound auditor" during Ubico's dictatorship and had orders to punish public treasurers who were either over or under in their balances. (Obviously a confusion of names: during Ubico's era, there was a public accountant named Aquilino Tun, who drafted a proposal for new income tax legislation.) Sagastume also tells us that whenever someone was accused of being a criminal, Ubico's personal motto was: "Execute him. We'll find out later."

Possible expressions:
Historical sadism. Sadistic realism.

Third Notebook: White Cover

Evening.

"The sultan did not really want Shahrazad to tell him stories; he was no doubt the one telling stories to her," Borges once told Bioy. Something similar happens to me now that I have become a regular at the Archive. I talk about that to B+ at all times—at dinner, while walking, or while staring at cracks in the plaster on the ceiling of my room. I tell her what I have seen there, what I have read—records and more records, identifying traits in a long series of obscure lives. That is to say, I bore her.

Power, as Borges says, always acts according to its own logic. The only possible criticism of this power is perhaps History. But since History is written from the present, and thus *encompasses it*, it is not probable that an impartial critique can be made.

I commit to reading, or at least thumbing through, Guatemalan "period" authors: for example, the "Generation of 1920," to which Asturias belonged.

February 5, 2007.

Cloudy day. I'm alone on the second floor of the Archive, alone with Sandra Gil and the policewoman watching over us. Radio music: "Lying Eyes." Sandra gives me a 1961 document that I did not ask for. She says that it may interest me: "Branch Inspector's Record Book." I take a quick look at it—nothing noteworthy.

Suddenly, I wonder what kind of Minotaur can hide in a

labyrinth like this one. It may be a hereditary trait to believe that every labyrinth has its Minotaur. If this one did not have its own, I might be tempted to invent one.

I continue to browse Yearly Reports. Clerk Tun was in charge of the 1939 edition. In addition to the police reports from various departments, the series for that year includes "A Pro-Police Apologia" by Gregorio Marañón and a text titled "In Praise of Fouché" (anonymous, but I sense penned by Tun himself).

Afternoon.
In the volumes for the years 1937, 1939, 1940, 1941, and 1943, I discover that the pages for the reports from the Bureau have been ripped out. I alert Sandra Gil about this, as well as the archivist on duty who delivered the mutilated volumes to me.

Tuesday.
In the Yearly Report from 1944 (published in January 1945, during the Revolutionary Government), I read the following in Chapter XXVIII, corresponding to the Identification Bureau: "This Bureau was, as in previous years, led by clerk Tun, who collaborated with tireless dedication and efficiency on the investigation of various criminal acts."
And further down, this letter from clerk Tun:

Guatemala, January 22, 1945
Mr. Director General of the Civil Guard, Delivered by Hand. Before providing specifics, which detail and demonstrate the efforts of the Identification Bureau under my leadership this past year of 1944, I deem it appropriate to expose, more justifiably

than ever now that a new era is opening up for our country and we move toward the implantation of democratic norms, what the Identification Bureau's work is within the organizational structure of the police.

The work of the Identification Bureau covers two broad areas. One concerns the human matter that enters Police Headquarters day after day for crimes or serious misdemeanors, and who need to be identified by means of the record card, which constitutes, so to speak, the first page in their criminal record, where the details of all future recidivism will appear. The other area where this Bureau acts is in matters pertaining to the laboratories of the Department of Technical Investigations itself: that is to say, the investigation by scientific means known today for the purpose of, on the one hand, identifying a criminal by the traces he might leave in places where he operates, and on the other hand, once identified or captured, furnishing evidence of his guilt.

Wednesday, February 7, 2007.

Today archivists on the second floor listen to salsa music. They give me more Yearly Reports to read. I find more mutilated pages (almost always in the pages corresponding to the report from the Identification Bureau, and rarely in other sections).

In the Yearly Report from 1938, a whole chapter, Chapter XI, is devoted to cases of folk medicine and witchcraft.

Thursday.

Pop music in Spanish: Arjona, Jarabe de Palo, Juanes, Manu Chao.

During the midmorning break, a female archivist, young and funny, who had spoken to me about my books on two or three occasions, approaches me to tell me that she is digitizing a series of "action radiograms"—stenographic copies of communications between police dispatch centers and patrol cars—dated 1970. She shows me one on the sly, which I copy immediately.

Guatemala, 7/4/70

It is possible that as a consequence of the accusations made in Escuintla by Pedro Matus, the police carried out a house search near Escuintla. There was resistance from the people in it, a total of six, who, protected by their weapons, took off to the hills. The police only found a young man in the house, about 19 to 22 years old, tall, blonde, who was arrested without offering resistance. Along the way, near San Andrés Villa Seca, he indicated that they would not get anything out of him, and that they might as well save themselves the trouble and kill him off, which "special" police Prudencio Aguirre did, shooting him between the eyes. This was witnessed by Colonel Carlos Sandoval, Head of the National Police of Escuintla, who finished him off with 14 shots from a .30 caliber gun.

The corpse was left hidden in the underbrush. Aguirre has been a bodyguard for several "anti-communist" leaders.

After the break, I ask Sandra if I could see those documents once they have been cataloged.

I start to get bored from looking through Yearly Reports. I snoop around the library, I kill time, while waiting for permission to see the documents I have requested, and especially the radiograms.

Document 1415 (requested at random):
Telegraphic codes of the National Police

Orders:

RABUA: I require from you immediate capture and safe delivery of . . .

RAFUD: due to lack of merit from the actions requested, cancel the order to capture . . .

ROGUE: report criminal records on . . .

Crimes:

DABUB: prosecuted for homicide

DAFUF: for threats

DEHOH: for fraud

DEGOG: for abduction

DIBIB: attempted murder

DOXEX: infanticide

General:

GADRO: known thief

GECHE: curly black hair

GISBI: well dressed

GISMA: dresses poorly

GISET: sex worker

GULGA: thin body

KABAB: proceed actively to their capture

KIFUZ: criminal was captured

VERAP: substitute will arrive

VIVAR: proceed tomorrow without fail

VOMIF: went today to . . .

VUMAG: sailed today for . . .

ZAHOH: for having venereal disease

ZAJUN: expel him from the country the way he came in

ZAGAB: you are no bother

ZEGUC: look closely

ZUVIV: it is not possible to meet your request

Lunch break.

While I eat lunch at El Altuna with Lucía Morán, I get a call from the chief:

"Where are you?"

"Having lunch."

"Are you inside, or outside [of the Archive]?"

"Outside, but nearby," I say.

"Very good. What I want to tell you would best be said in person, but I'm leaving on a trip tomorrow and I will not be back for ten days. A problem has come up. You have to suspend your visits. Do not return to the Archive, please," he tells me.

"Agreed. I hope it's nothing serious."

"I'll call you when I get back. Bye."

I hang up and, through the window, I see a trio of school-girls in uniform, leaving the high school across the street. They roll up their checkered skirts at the waist, giving them two or three turns and making them into miniskirts—quite provocative.

"What happened?" Lucía asks.

I stop looking out the window. I have the fleeting thought that perhaps it is a lucky thing not to have to return to the Archive.

"They just suspended me," I say.

"Why?"

"In ten, maybe eleven days, I'll find out."

I have not stopped wondering what the reason could be for my suspension. Could it have to do with the pages torn from the Yearly Reports? Or was it my request to see the action radiograms? Or perhaps, though less likely, was it the "unfriendly" question that I asked Dr. Novales at his lecture series in the Ciudad Vieja? In any case, my interest in the Archive as novelistic material, which was beginning to fade, has now been reawakened because of this call.

Second Sketchbook: Don Quixote

Such is the spirit of the human heart: where it finds the most resistance, it is there that it tends to put the most effort.

Friday.

First visit to the General Archives of Central America (whose long gray exterior walls are impregnated with the smell of urine from countless incontinent citizens), in search of more Yearly Reports by the National Police, while my "suspension" lasts.

Me: Visitor number 13.

I come across a curious coincidence: in the old and rustic filing cabinet of the library at the General Archives, the Yearly Reports are missing for the years that interest me: 1937, 1939, 1940, 1941, and 1943, the ones where the chapters for the Identification Bureau were missing.

I requested to see Yearly Reports for other years, and the woman in charge served me with two whole boxes containing the decades 1930–1950. And that is where I found the volumes I had been seeking, which did not appear in the card catalog, and whose pages for the Identification Bureau had not been mutilated. I asked them to make me photocopies of the pages that were missing from the Police Archive, even before reading their contents.

Second visit. Monday.

While I wait for the librarian to deliver more volumes to me, I leaf through an issue from the Gazette of the Police dated October 15, 1944 (five days after the Guatemalan Revolution). I am struck by the picture of a French reporter.

A slain soldier, his hands tied to a post, has been shot by a

55

firing squad for treason. Another soldier, his arm outstretched, revolver in hand, is leaning next to him. ("Coup-de-grace in Grenoble, France," reads the caption.)

Upon turning the page: "Louis Renault, car manufacturer, arrested in Fresnes prison, accused of collaborating with the Nazis."

Tuesday.

I visit the Library of Congress. On the street, on the sidewalk, congressmen come and go. Physically, they look like Guatemalan peasants, but they are dressed in three-piece formal suits, wearing designer sunglasses, and accompanied by men who look like them, bodyguards who have something of a cowboy air about them. Here and there, interspersed with the diesel smell of pickup trucks, you sense the strong smell of expensive perfume, or perhaps of a knockoff.

The Library of Congress is a nice place, cool and quiet. They tell me they do not have Yearly Reports from the police, that the library was destroyed by fire about twenty years ago and that few volumes survived the flames. They let me consult the card catalogs. I ask for several books.

From *Justo Rufino Barrios Face-to-Face with Posterity* (A. Díaz):

Names of criminals and known gangs in the New City of Guatemala at the end of the nineteenth century, when the National Police was founded (1881):

The Chicharrones
The Contingencies
The Gentle One
The Marimberos
The Roldans

El Tucurú (Ricardo Rodríguez), "the first prisoner executed by firing squad in the New City of Guatemala."

Other "causes célèbres":

The unresolved mystery of the Chinese man, Mariano Ching, who had his throat cut and was emasculated in his bed (1935).

The case of the beheaded woman (1945).

José María Miculax Bux, confessed rapist and strangler of twelve "white children" between the ages of ten and sixteen. Originally from San Andrés, Patzicía, he committed his crimes around Antigua and the New City of Guatemala. He was a survivor of the Patzicía massacre, which was shortly after the Kaqchikel uprising that was due to land problems; the government, in order to repress the uprising, sent in 1944 a punitive expedition that ended the lives of about a thousand indigenous peoples—among them, apparently, the parents and siblings of the young Miculax. Executed by firing squad in 1946 at the age of twenty-one. His skull is still preserved as a subject of (Lombrosian?) study at the School of Criminology at San Carlos University.

Saturday. Lake Atitlán. Evening.

In the morning, before going to pick up Pía at her mother's, I asked B+ to call the number that I found in the phone book under the name of Benedicto Tun, a possible descendant of the Bureau's director. I now call her from the hotel, to see if she has any news. The Benedicto Tun of the phone book is the son of the former, who was head of the Identification Bureau. B+ had a fairly long conversation with him, she tells me. On my instructions, she told him that she was working on a university thesis on the history of the National Police.

In principle, Tun is willing to talk about his father. B+ tells me that he is a bit annoyed at the state for the way they treated his father at the time of his retirement. When he requested his retirement, in 1964, he was given a pension of one hundred and twenty quetzals a month, which even then was a small amount. But he did not cash in on that pension because he continued to work. In 1970 he suffered brain trauma, which resulted in him giving up his job. They increased his pension a little, based on a decree-law by the military government of Peralta Azurdia. Then, the Bureau underwent some modifications; the divisions for criminology, ballistics, and graphology were separated, and in a few years the name of Benedicto Tun fell into oblivion. The son also told B+ that he keeps some official documents, rescued from the various raids and searches that the police conducted in his home after the death of his father.

After a few months of working at the Archive, every time I talk on the phone (especially on the cell phone), I think I may be listened to. Something the chief said the other day about it not being advisable to discuss my suspension over the phone reinforces my suspicion. So, I tell B+ that we better talk about this when I return to the capital.

Pía, who has been playing with her paints while I was talking, asks me:

"Who was it?"

I tell her:

"Beatriz" (which is also the name of her godmother). "But not *your* Beatriz."

"Why is her name Beatriz?"

I laughed.

"How old is she?"

"About forty."

"Forty!" Pía exclaimed, and kept playing and stopped asking.

Tuesday.

I call Benedicto Tun from a pay phone. His voice is that of a sixty-year-old man, perhaps a bit older. He is a criminal lawyer, and yes, he is willing to talk to me about his father. His voice sounds happy when he talks about the old man. "At one point, around 1961 or 1962, we thought about starting a private research laboratory together. I wanted him to leave the Bureau, but he kept postponing and postponing his retirement. Finally, when he actually retired, at seventy-four, we set up the laboratory. He died ten years later." He mentions again the pension that his father received when he retired, and the lack of recognition by the government and the National Police for his work and career.

"That's how the state has behaved with men like him. I was a little hurt, I can't lie to you," he says.

I tell him that it seems natural to me.

"I have a few things, but just scraps," he continues to say, "of what he left written, apart from what he wrote for the Yearly Reports. I believe that he had even started writing his personal memoirs, but there is very little of that, because of the accident."

He asks me for a number so that he can call me when he finds those papers.

"Although I don't know if they will be of any use for what you say you are writing," he adds.

I explain that I would like to write a history of the Guatemalan police in the twentieth century, and I think that his father's biography could possibly serve as a connecting thread.

We agree to talk again in the near future to arrange for an interview.

Monday, February 26.

The front pages of today's newspapers report the death of four high-ranking police officers. The policemen had been imprisoned two or three days earlier, charged with "credible" evidence, for the brutal murder of three Salvadoran congressmen and their driver, about thirty kilometers from Guatemala City on February 19 of this year.

The chief of the Archive Recovery Project, who returned from his trip a few days ago, had given me an appointment at the Ombudsman's Office to speak about my suspension. Before leaving my home, I call to confirm our appointment.

"I've hit a snag, my friend," he says. "A friend of my children was killed in an accident yesterday. They crashed on the road to Totonicapán. Everyone in the car died. A tragedy. I'm at the cemetery."

He gives me another appointment for tomorrow at three.

Tuesday.

Ombudsman's Office. It's almost four in the afternoon, and I'm still waiting for the chief. One of his assistants just told me he's on his way, but caught in a traffic jam. While I wait, I read the press and I take notes.

"Gang of policemen suspected of a crime against Salvadoran congressmen could have at least 12 members.

"February 19: The burned remains of Salvadoran congressmen to the Central American Parliament were found, along with their car and driver. Three days later, four agents belonging to the Office of Criminal Investigations were captured for the murder of the Salvadoran congressmen. They were sent to jail in Zone 18 by order of a judge; that same day they were transferred to the high security prison El Boquerón (Santa Rosa), where there are individual cells. However, the four agents were locked up in the same cell. Two days later, the four policemen were mysteriously executed in their cell."

I see the wall clock; I decide to wait another fifteen minutes. However, the fifteen minutes go by and I do not get up. I must get an explanation about my suspension, I tell myself. I wait until five. The chief does not arrive.

Wednesday.

Two days ago—I read in today's newspapers—there was an enormous collapse of land in Zone 6, where the Archive is located. "At least three people were swallowed by the earth and about 300 had to vacate their homes. In the last few hours, more residents had to abandon their homes when they heard the ground rumble."

Apparently the "San Antonio Sinkhole," a kind of cenote with a diameter of fifty meters and sixty meters deep, endangers not only the surrounding homes but also the facilities where the Archive is located, only 185 meters away. Yesterday, the press reports, the directors of the Archive Recovery Project discussed the imminent removal of the documents to keep them safe.

In part, that explains why the chief did not come to our last appointment. I decide to be patient.

Midday. Francisco Marroquín University Library. Nothing about the history of the police.

I browse texts at random. Cesare Beccaria:

In politics, the one who reaps is not always the one who sowed.

Lawmakers should direct public happiness. They should; that is, they do not.

All punishment that does not derive from absolute necessity is tyrannical.

Any man is at a certain moment the center of all the permutations on the globe.

Afternoon.

In the anthology of essays *Intellectual History of Guatemala* (Marta Casaús Arzú, 2001) that a young archivist lent me, I read:

Roger de Lyss, *New Times*, Guatemala, 1924:

The Indian cannot be a citizen. As long as the Indian is a citizen, we Guatemalans will not be free. Those poor wretches have been born slaves, they carry that in their blood, it is the heritage of centuries, the cursed fate that the conquistador imposed on them.

Benedicto Tun, who was the son of an Indian father and mother, created the Identification Bureau in 1922.

Thursday.

The chief again gave me an appointment at the offices of the Human Rights Ombudsman. And again, he was a no-show. I talk to him on the phone, I tell him that first of all I would like to know the reason for my suspension. He tells me he cannot go into details over the phone, but that the day they suspended me there was a general meeting, and "someone" said that I asked to see a box with radiograms of actions from the 1970s. Revealing these documents to me right away (the day they were found) would have violated, apparently, some confidentiality rule. The chief says he cannot explain anything else to me by phone, but not to worry, that it's just a misunderstanding, that I will be able to go back to the Archive. We agree on a new appointment for next week.

Friday.

I return to visit the General Archive of Central America. I leaf through more National Police Yearly Reports. I ask for photocopies, which will not be delivered to me until Monday. I also request a university thesis on the police, which they will also let me read on Monday.

From the press:

"Today another agent sought for the murder of the Salvadoran congressmen voluntarily turned himself in to the authorities."

Afternoon. Francisco Marroquín University Library.

Voltaire: *The need to talk, the difficulty of having nothing to say, and the desire to be witty are three things capable of making the greatest man ridiculous.*

Saturday.

The phone stared ringing at about two o'clock in the morning. I got up to answer, but there was no one on the line. This happened again at least five times. I figure it was a mistake, perhaps mistaken programming from some wake-up call service. Aside from that, a quiet Saturday. Pía and I had lunch at my parents'. We spent the afternoon at María Marta's, the second of my sisters. I tried to read a bit while Pía watched a movie (*The Pacifier*). We had pizza delivered at home.

"Every text is ambiguous," I say out loud, half asleep. I believe it.

Monday.

Telephone call from Oaxaca, Mexico. I'm invited to a roundtable of "international writers"—among them, my friend Homero Jaramillo.

Benedicto Tun has not called, as he said he would, once he had organized the papers from his father that he wanted to show me.

I read "A Defense of Ardor" by Zagajewski, the Polish writer that Homero recommended to me a few days ago in an email. He seems all right to me, but he does not quite convince me, as Dr. Aguado would say. It is true that I do not know many of the authors that he quotes, and that diminishes my reading.

The question that I think I should be asking myself about Tun and his work at the National Police is this: in such an environment, could he have been a decent man, or even more than that, an *exemplary* man?

It is necessary, says Pascal, *that we explain to ourselves the amazing contradictions that conjugate in us.*

Voltaire: *There are no contradictions in us, or in nature, in general. What we find everywhere are inconveniences.*

It occurs to me to go to Opus Magnum, the tailor shop, with the pretext of getting a suit made. I would like to talk with the owner, a former schoolmate of mine as well as brother of one of the police officers whose name has been in the newspapers lately, in connection with the crime that people call "the Salvadoran pork roast," and who, as a result of this, has just resigned. Jaime Gonzales, the police officer and my tailor's brother, graduated as a doctor in 1989, and practiced in the Police Hospital between 1991 and 1997. According to some reporters and columnists, he always had a reputation for being violent. I would like to ask the tailor what he thinks of this rumor. And if he knows why his brother decided to become a policeman.

Let us find comfort in not knowing what connections might exist between a spider and a ring of Saturn and let us continue instead to examine what is within our reach.—Voltaire.

Who was that contemporary of Asturias who argued that in order to think up a nation-building project valid for Guatemala it would be necessary to allow the indigenous people to become full citizens, not deprived of their rights as they were then—and in many cases, still are today? I fail to remember his name, and yet he did exist, that contemporary writer or historian *unfairly forgotten.* He is one of a few authors whom I have read who is not seduced by the idea of a "eugenic nation" and the absurd project of "importing European blood to improve the race," advocated by Miguel Ángel Asturias.

Email from Homero Jaramillo, who asks me for a letter of recommendation for an asylum program in Canada. He attached this:

Case H. Jaramillo.

Date of threat: November 2005.

Nature of threat: Two midnight phone calls to my parent's house, where I used to live, saying that I was going to be killed because of what I wrote in my book Profiles of the Underground *published a few days before the threats.*

Identity of persons carrying out threat: Anonymous. They did not identify themselves.

I write this letter, or rather, I recycle it, because I have already used the text on another occasion:

Dear Sirs at Canadian Cities of Asylum,

This letter is to attest that I am aware that Mr. Jaramillo has been the object of death threats in his country. I am also aware that his very critical views on the political state of affairs in Honduras has made him enemies on all sides, a situation which would make it very difficult to work in his field at the present moment in Central America. As you may know, in places like Honduras, El Salvador, and Guatemala, where Mr. Jaramillo has worked in the past, the practice of silencing enemies—political or other—by death threats or, in many cases, by death, has again become commonplace.

Monday at noon.

The chief just called me to, once again, postpone our meeting. He assures me, however, that he is still interested, and still believes in the work that "we could do." He tells me that he will call later so that we can agree on another appointment.

I call again, and I finally find Tun. He explains to me that the number I dialed a few days ago is the one in his office, but the call has been forwarded to his cell phone; he is out on the street and cannot talk. He asks me to call him later, around six. I agree to call him tomorrow at nine.

After lunch I go to the General Archive to pick up the photocopies, which are ready; not so the thesis. I'm asked to come back for it tomorrow, Tuesday.

Front page today: "High-ranking police chief leaves the country." This is Jaime Gonzales, a former student at Liceo

Javier high school. He left with his wife and children on a flight to Costa Rica. The "brief note" in *Prensa Libre* says: "Who is Jaime Gonzales? Profession: Doctor and surgeon. He joined the National Civil Police in 2005 as deputy director of health. Three months later he was appointed deputy general manager, in charge of the Division of Investigations. He was the boss of Victor Soto, one of the agents executed in El Boquerón.

"Passengers aboard the TACA 911 flight bound for Costa Rica described Gonzales as not having the beard and mustache that he used to have and that he no doubt shaved off in order to go unnoticed. They also reported that, when he went through the boarding gate, the former official carried a baby, only a few months old, in his arms. His wife and other children, aged nine and four, followed him. Gonzales and his family were picked up in San José by a private tourist service (although they had no reservations on the TACA flight that they took) and they did not say where they were going. Asked whether he left Guatemala out of fear, the former police chief shook his head and continued walking. Pro-justice advocacy groups of course lamented that the former official left the country before clarifying the involvement of the police group under his charge in the crime against the burned Salvadorans. They also expressed their surprise that no judge with authority had issued a travel restriction against Gonzales in the midst of the current scandal."

Evening.

A bit bored at first and then with surprise, I read an email from Tracy Veal, whom I have not seen in several years, and who now lives in New York. It contains links to two press articles: one about the recent police-related events that have put Guatemala back in the pages of the *New York Times*, another from the *Guardian Weekly* about the Archive.

The *Guardian*: *"The Archive sits in a former police base in Guatemala City, ringed by razor wire and a 24-hour armed guard. We were allowed access on condition we did not identify any of the 100 investigators working here. . . . The person in overall charge of the Ombudsman's inquiry says there is psychological pressure on these workers, who know their lives may be at risk due to the political sensitivity of their work. He has received numerous death threats. There are some extremely 'unhappy people' in the higher echelons of government and the army—he says. And people still go missing here in Guatemala."*

I imagine the "unhappy people" referred to in the article are wishing that the San Antonio sinkhole would somehow swallow the Archive.

Fourth Notebook: Red and Blue Stripes on a White Background

Nighttime.

Slightly disappointed: Benedicto did not call me, nor did the chief.

I return to the General Archive of Central America. They give me the thesis: *History of the National Police of Guatemala, 1881–1997* (University of San Carlos, 2004), by one José Adolfo C. Cruz. This revives me—before I start reading.

I browse the thesis: big disappointment. Was this done by the son of a policeman?—that is the question this sleepy reader asks himself.

The bibliography does not include any of the thirty-plus volumes of Yearly Reports by the National Police, nor any issues of the famous *Police Gazette*.

From the "List of directors of the National Police," I highlight:

Mario Méndez Montenegro.

Antonio Estrada Sanabria (horse-riding friend of my father's).

Wednesday.

Today at seven in the evening, at the Center for Hispanic Culture at Cuatro Grados Norte, presentation of my little novel *Caballeriza*. Even though I do not want to go, I will. This part of the work, a presentation to the press or to the public ("that monster," as W. H. Auden would say), is for me the most uncomfortable and the least pleasant; and in the case of this "realistic" story told in the first person, the discomfort is magnified.

Late at night.

"No one can express themselves entirely in art," someone said. And I add: *nor in reality.*

Regarding my words during the presentation (I think I said that the little novel, written more than two years ago, no longer seemed at all daring, as it seemed to me when I was writing it): the husband of the editor (who is a good friend of mine) ruled: *Bad marketing.*

Thursday.

Neither the chief nor Tun have called. I feel tired, as if empty, after the presentation. Too much drinking as well. Today it does not seem possible to do anything with joy. In the afternoon I'll go pick up Pía so she can sleep over. By then I hope to be in better spirits.

Too many upcoming trips are piling up on me, and I feel it: Petén tomorrow afternoon, Oaxaca on the sixteenth, France in early April.

Sunday. Hotel Villa Maya, Santa Elena, Petén.

While I shower before embarking on the return trip to Guatemala City, I remember the conversation we had at dinner after the presentation of *Cabelleriza* at La Casa del Águila. I was at a dinner that included my eldest sister, Magalí, an environmental activist branded an "ecoterrorist" by a number of newspaper columnists; a friend of hers who worked as a driver for a guerrilla organization, who today makes a career as an advisor to political parties, and his wife; and Willy Sprighmul, a former classmate at Liceo Javier high school, who has become a prominent businessman in the frozen food import-export business. Among other things, we talked of my work (suspended) at the Archive. Magalí and her friends were aware of it, but I had to explain to Willy what the Archive was and what I was doing there. Willy's overall response was one of astonishment.

"Very well," he then said, not only to me but to the table in general, "but what's the point of digging into the past? It is better to let the dead rest in peace, right?"

His reasoning resembles that of my father, and reminds me of an after-dinner conversation that I recently had with him. I had just explained that my original intention in requesting access to the Archive had been to investigate cases of artists and intellectuals persecuted or recruited by the police, but that given the state of disarray of the documents and the time that would be required to catalog them, this had turned out to be impossible.

"And so?" my father asked.

"I have been allowed to see other things," I explained. "There are a number of documents from something called the Identification Bureau, led for several decades by a certain Benedicto Tun . . ."

"And that interests you?"

"Yes, I find it interesting."

"So," my father concluded, "your interest degenerated."

I had to laugh and tell him that that was partly right.

Monday. Stop in Cobán.

In a way, reviewing history is dealing with the dead. We do not read history; we always reread it, as we reread the classics, according to Borges. Before reading it, we have a general idea of what it will say.

Like Zagajewski in his "Intellectual Krakow," I saw the Archive as a place where the stories of the dead were in the air like filaments of strange plasma, a place where one could get a glimpse of some "spectacular machines of terror," like stage machinery that has been hidden from view. I wonder: Might other researchers see something else?

This is also from Zagajewski:

To describe new varieties of good and evil—there lies the great task of the writer—and, now he does convince me, in an essay titled "Against Poetry."

To describe new varieties . . . And what if the new varieties were to *obliterate* the old ideas about good and evil, of what one or the other can be or become in each person's subjectivity?

Even the best of us—and I am thinking of "us" in the widest possible sense—needs to constantly choose between good and evil. Then, it becomes obvious that the choices are never identical, nor can they be, between two different people, because their circumstances—of time and place at the very least—are necessarily different. Time and place: both concepts are understood in their entirety—that is, in their tendency to infinity.

Poetry, that little grain of ecstasy that changes the flavor of the Universe, Zagajewski writes.

Saturday morning.

On my reading desk—a low table of Kaqchikel craftsmanship—I have a number of the photocopies of the Police Yearly Reports that were made at the General Archive of Central America. I see three photographs of the woman "known as Angela Fuentes when she was alive" and her remains. The caption under the first photo reads: "The macabre torso being examined by the coroner in the anatomical theater." (The title of the article, which comes from the previous page, is "The Monstrous Crime of Majadas, or the Beheaded Woman.") The caption for another photo, showing the skull, reads: "The detached head was found 200 meters from the body." Date: November 20, 1945. The author of the article: Benedicto Tun.

Tuesday the 13th.

At about eleven o'clock I call Benedicto, the son, again. He apologizes for not calling a few days ago, as he had agreed to do, and tells me that he has found more documents that could be of use to me. He proposes that we meet further down the line, in order to come to an agreement as to what documents I will use, and how. We agree to talk again tonight at seven o'clock.

Later, I call the chief. He also apologizes, and "so as not to further delay our meeting," he gives me an appointment for tomorrow afternoon at two, after lunch, at the cafe next to Taco Bell on Avenida de las Américas.

Nighttime.

I definitely want to go back to the Archive. I want to see the place again, with its army of researchers that make me think of Kafka characters, with their outlandish clothes, their piercings and tattoos under their ocher-colored lab coats with optimistic bright green badges that say "Archive Recovery Project": the older folk, with gray hair and stooped shoulders, and the frustrated revolutionaries who work there for the salary but also diligently, with a kind of dull determination, because they want to make the dead speak. I could almost guarantee that, as in my case, no one (except perhaps the cleaning crew and the accountants) is there completely disinterestedly or innocently. Everyone there, in some way, files and records documents *in favor of* or *against* their own interest, with anticipation, and perhaps sometimes with fear as well. Nobody knows, as they say, whom they work for, and even less whom they have worked for.

Wednesday, March 21, afternoon.

"When you get back from Oaxaca," the chief said to me, "you can go back to visiting the Archive." I must call him upon my return.

During our last interview, I made the blunder of not letting him finish telling me about his children's friend who had died a few days before in a traffic accident in Totonicapán: something about the bonds of friendship that united them, from their childhood in a "beehive"—which was the term used to refer to the shelters for the children of members of the Guerrilla Army of the Poor.

Here, a comment of mine made the conversation shift toward the business of illegal adoptions. According to the chief, it began in the eighties and was linked to massacres in the countryside, especially in the western highlands. Although at first the normal procedure was to leave no survivors, later the soldiers began to leave the children alive, who were then taken to the so-called newborn shelters.

I asked if he thought that they stopped killing children due to some humanitarian scruple. He said he did not think so, that they had realized that "it could be very good business, putting them up for sale for adoption."

After I updated him on my findings regarding the Identification Bureau, the chief told me that he liked the idea of focusing on a character like Tun instead of on a "psychopath" like Barnabas Linares (alias *Linduras*), of whom he had spoken—known as one of the biggest thugs serving Ubico and subsequent counterrevolutionary governments.

He also explained details of the "misunderstanding" that caused the suspension of my visits to the Archive. He spoke of resentments, of "channels"; issues of confidentiality and professional jealousy; security issues. It was not advisable, for example, when referring to what I was doing at the Archive, to use the word "research." No one, other than the team from the Ombudsman's Office proper, had the authority to carry out any kind of research there. Among the team members, there were students majoring in history, political science, and law who had requested permission to use documents from the Archive for their theses or fieldwork, and all requests had been denied by the chief. I enjoyed a simple privilege, he said, adding: "I granted it to you based on an intuition, and I may be wrong, since I don't know you, and we are not friends."

An intuition: that the result of my work as a writer could help the nonspecialized public to know about the Archive Recovery Project and allow them to realize the importance of such a find.

Wednesday the 28th, evening.
Strange day, empty.

Thursday.
An even emptier day, if that's possible, than yesterday—due to last night's excess of red wine and Spanish brandy. I took a nap at my parents' house. While I rested, I thought about my mother, who is almost ninety years old and who spends a good part of her days sleeping in one of the rooms with large windows overlooking a large garden shaded by old trees.

At seven Magalí called. My mother must be hospitalized right away. She needs a kidney drainage. Apparently one of her kidneys had not been working for several months, perhaps years.

We accompany her to the hospital. My niece Claudia, Magalí's eldest, will spend the night with her.

Saturday. I fly to Oaxaca.

On the plane I read a news article on state-sponsored terrorism in Guatemala, "Heritage or Fate?," penned by an influential columnist. I clip the article and mark this passage in red ink:

Exasperated and exalted by the paradise that common criminals and organized crime enjoy at their leisure, the highest echelons of Security and the Guatemalan State have always opted for efficiency and pragmatism and have proceeded to organize death squads composed of police officers and professional hitmen hired to kill criminals. These extrajudicial practices are popular causes, as the vast majority of Guatemalans are vulnerable and defenseless against crime and are convinced that for ruthless criminals there is no other way than to give them a taste of their own medicine. In other words, despair and fear among the citizenry ends up granting a certain legitimacy to this variation of state-sponsored terrorism.

I wonder if the columnist counts himself among those who believe that this "variation of state-sponsored terrorism" does, in fact, have any legitimacy.

No one will ever know with certainty—he continues, and now seems to want to revise the most recent history—*who, among the thousands fallen during three decades of war, was guilty or innocent, nor how many were slain by the insurgency or by the counterinsurgency.*

"What about forensic medicine?" I wonder.

"Why don't you tell him to look at the work of Clyde Snow or Michael Ondaatje?" said an old Mexican poet when I told him about this in the arid outskirts of Oaxaca.

From the Internet: *"Clyde Snow was appointed by President George Bush (senior) to be part of the Human Rights Commission at the United Nations in 1991. Considered an "international popular hero" in forensic anthropology, Snow has selected paradigmatic cases of Guatemalan massacres to establish precedents in cases of 'atrocities' against human rights. According to his reports, more than one hundred thousand people were killed by members of the Guatemalan army between 1960 and 1996, and about ten thousand by the various guerrilla groups in the same period."*

Sunday, in Oaxaca.

Yesterday afternoon, reading of my stories in San Agustín Etla in an old textile mill converted into a cultural center, in the middle of a wild landscape of gray mountains and dark blue sky. By late afternoon, incredibly drunk on mezcal. At night, a rush of visions and memories.

My mother was kidnapped in Guatemala City on June 28, 1981, and released on December 23 of that same year. We never got to know who held her during those six months, and, in fact, no one in the family wanted to carry out any kind of investigation. In the beginning we speculated that her kidnappers were criminal members of the government or of the National Police. (Back in those years it was not uncommon for parties or political factions to kidnap in order to finance their electoral campaigns or war strategies, or just to get rich.) One of the signs that supported this hypothesis was something that happened during the delivery of the ransom. My uncle, the doctor Eduardo García-Salas, and I were designated to deliver the money. We had to go the typical route in the style of "a treasure hunt" through Guatemala City, a journey that started at about four in the morning, in complete darkness. At a given moment, we were instructed to leave the car that we were driving in a public parking lot and to get in another vehicle that was already there, a blue Datsun pickup, that year's model. There was an envelope in the glove compartment with further instructions: "Remove all of your clothing outside the pickup, under the streetlight next to you, and put on the gym clothes that are under the seat . . ." In addition to the instructions, we found the car registration and deed in the glove compartment. To our surprise, they were made out in my name, and carried the seal of the National Police and the signature of the deputy director.

The delivery took place without any setbacks and that very afternoon my mother was safely at home, although weak. She had lost about fifty pounds in captivity. A priest who was a friend of the family drove her. It was near his parish that the kidnappers set my mother free, and it was through him that my father had first received communication about the kidnapping, six months earlier.

A few days after her liberation, my mother ordered a mass of thanksgiving, where she made public her desire for her kidnappers to be forgiven by the powers of this world "and the world beyond." Within the family circle, the criminal aspect of the case was forgotten. Other than the financial fallout resulting from the ransom payment, my father's premature gray hair, and the breakdown suffered by my youngest sister, Mónica, (no doubt the greatest damage), the family was practically unscathed. And I daresay this experience was in a certain way enriching for my mother, then sixty-four, putting her in touch with unexpected reserves of inner strength. She gained a broader social conscience, and, after the kidnapping, she became a kinder woman.

For several years, I thought that one of the gangs under the leadership of Donaldo Álvarez Ruiz, who at the time was minister of the Interior and is today a fugitive from justice and wanted by Interpol, was responsible for the kidnapping. However, about twelve or thirteen years later, we received information that made us change our minds, and we came up with a different hypothesis about the identity of the kidnappers. In 1994 I resettled in Guatemala after almost fifteen years of voluntary exile, and among the new friends I had, there were some ex-guerrilla fighters. One day, during a long conversation over drinks, one of them assured me that my mother's kidnappers were members of an urban guerrilla group, short-lived and practically unknown, that carried the name "January 18th Movement," and whose founder and ringleader, Eugenio Camposeco, died in an automobile accident in 1982. I must say that the possibility that my mother's kidnappers were guerrillas and not policemen was unpleasant for me because, although I never had direct links with any of the revolutionary organizations, I sympathized with them and not with the government—and this fact made it unavoidable to recognize that, ideology aside, there were "natural enemies" among the ranks of the insurgents. And then, the day before my trip, one of my female friends, who was part of the "support team" for a guerrilla organization, told me that there was a rumor, among several archivists, that the reason I was there was that I was searching for the identity of my mother's kidnappers, who might very well be employees at the Archive Recovery Project.

My suspension—I now wonder—was it not due to that?

Wednesday morning.

An unforgettable nightmare last night, returning from Oaxaca. B+ came to pick me up at the airport. She stayed with me a while and shortly after one o'clock (my flight had arrived close to midnight) she went home, half asleep, to go back to bed. I stayed up a while reading emails, then went to bed, too. A little while later, the phone rang. I got up to answer: nothing. I went back to bed and fell asleep.

I woke up at four, drenched in sweat and overcome with an intense fear. It was not a violent dream, but what I would call an authentic ghost dream. B+ and I were at my parents', in my parents' bedroom, next to the French door that leads to the garden. From the colors—the green reflections of the grass and the almost black-green of the leaves on the trees (trembling in the dream), I knew it was late in the day. There was a strange noise in the back of the house, near the hallway that leads to the living room. As I listened, I heard demented laughter that seemed to come from the kitchen. B+ was very frightened. She asked: "What was that?" "Ghosts," I said. "That must be the laughter of a ghost, or someone who wants to frighten us."

I went to the hallway, where, all of a sudden, night had fallen and it was very dark. I stretched out my arm—I think I actually did this in bed, while sleeping—to turn on the light.

A little while ago I told B+ my dream. I told her that when I turned on the light, I woke up. But I withheld the ending, which was truly the terrifying part for me:

When I turn the light on, I see my father coming in from the balcony. He looks tired and is much thinner than in real life. He has something under his arm that I think is a bottle of beer, dark beer. I think: Then, it isn't him. (My father, to the best of my recollection, has never drunk dark beer.) Now the laughter is fainter. The man with the beer, who may or may not be my father, is impassive, as if he has not heard anything strange. He goes into a room and closes the door gently. I hear the click. And then, I wake up terrified, sweating, cold from the damp pajamas against my skin. I get up to change. I go back to bed and sleep without interruption until almost noon.

Thursday.

From the press: Social cleansing in Lake Atitlán. Armed groups (with names such as "Hitmen Without Borders") have carried out thirty-six executions in the last six months. Among the victims: thieves, witch doctors, unfaithful couples, drug addicts, and corrupt government employees. These "cleansing" groups (someone should coin a new term for this concept of *social cleansing*) publish lists with the names of their next victims. Residents accuse the Ministry of Justice of negligence.

A moment ago, I was looking for the manila envelope with the photocopies of the "elimination list" created by members of the army, which I obtained a few weeks ago from Luis Galíndez. As sometimes happens with a book or a document that I want to revisit or reread, that envelope is hidden, for now, in the usual mess of my papers. Instead, I find a binder, like the ones I used in school. It contains letters written by my maternal grandfather to his wife and children a few hours before his suicide. An airmail envelope has the following written on it: *For Doña Emigdia Monroy, Widow of García Salas.* In it there is a goodbye letter written by Don Jorge shortly before shooting himself in the chest. The letter ends: *Forgive me thus, and taking everything philosophically, looking for the best side of everything, I wish you all happiness. This is the last and most burning desire from someone who loved you with all his heart.*

There is also a forensic letter, explaining that the death of

Mr. García Salas "was produced by a gun shot from a revolver, whose projectile entered the thorax on the left, perforating the skin, cellular tissue, muscles, the lung, and the heart."

I give up my search for the lost envelope and continue to read documents from my grandfather, who wrote scientific articles on agriculture and agronomy—among them, several defenses of small farms (in opposition to the large plantations that dominated Guatemala)—during the 1910s, 1920s, and 1930s for several local newspapers, and the story of an expedition to the Petén jungle—which he led himself—to combat a plague of locusts, and which resulted in a confrontation with the authorities in Chiapas, Mexico, where the plague was successfully diverted from Petén by my grandfather.

My thoughts go back to the ghostly dream I had last night. Few dreams have left such a strong impression on me in the last few years; this is perhaps due to what I could call the careful cinematic realism of the production.

Friday.

I have a dream about my mother dying. She is in my arms, after a brief but intense agony. She has fallen on her back and hit her head. Just before, we were talking about one of my trips. Her skin color changes suddenly: it is bright, shiny, almost electric, and then, suddenly, it turns pale. She is completely nude, and her skin is ashen. Everything in her has darkened. This happens in the kitchen of her own house, next to the small table where Luisa, my parent's Tzutuhil servant, eats. I bend over to pick her up in my arms. In a few seconds she has lost a horrible amount of weight. I want to take her to the living room. I run into Magalí in the hallway and we get into an absurd argument about where we should lay her to rest. We decide to take her to her room. I keep talking to her, carrying her in my arms. She has closed her eyes. I say to her, "My love, my sweet love," and I know she is dying. By the time we arrive in her room, she has died. I wake up in sobs.

Midmorning.

I call Benedicto Tun again. He tells me he has found several rulings that he thinks might be of interest to me and several cassette tapes with something that his father was preparing for a *History of the National Police*. He suggests that we come up with a "firm plan": He gives me an appointment at his office for next Tuesday afternoon. He asks me if I can bring a cassette player, as he does not have one. After hanging up the phone, I go check; I have one in my studio that I could loan him.

I call the chief's cell phone. He does not answer, and his mailbox is full.

Afternoon.

I go pick up Pía from her catechism session at San Judas Tadeo church. There are a dozen bodyguards in the parking lot, who accompany four or five "anguished mothers" (two of them, stunning), who are also there to pick up their children.

At my parents', after lunch.

The press is carrying two news items related to the Archive and another one related to the National Civil Police.

1) One month after the "cave-in" in Zone 6, no one is taking responsibility for those who lost their homes, nor is there any support whatsoever for the relatives of the deceased. The sinkhole continues to widen and the danger continues to grow, affecting the buildings surrounding the Archive.

2) A committee has been established to support the National Police Archive Recovery Project. "The Human Rights Ombudsman awaits the files on cases of human rights violations during the internal conflict." "A. M. de Klein, member of the Anguished Mothers* organization, considered that the investment that must be made in order to catalog the approximately eighty million pages should be made instead in education and health, because the present is more important than scouring the past." On the other hand, Mrs. Verónica Godoy, a member of the Public Safety Support Group, says that "it is vital to recover our collective memory, so that we can see the modes of operation of the National Police, whose highest-ranking members are currently expected to testify before our courts."

3) Yesterday another officer of the National Civil Police was executed (extrajudicially) in connection with the murder

---

* Anguished Mothers (Madres Angustiadas) is an anti-violence group in support of women and families of victims of violent crimes.

of the Salvadoran congressmen and their driver. This was done by four young men under twenty years old, according to eyewitnesses, in front of Ríos de Agua Viva elementary school, owned and directed by the same police officer. "In the El Coco community, this man was known to be both a criminal and, at the same time, a police officer."

Third Sketchbook: "Scribe"

Friday morning.

I call the chief several times; mailbox full.

Prensa Libre carries more news and commentaries about the National Civil Police, publicly identified by the United Nations Special Rapporteur on Human Rights, Philip Alston, for carrying out "social cleansing" operations. The Rapporteur adds: "This is a good country in which to commit a crime."

I call the chief again; he does not answer.

Afternoon.

The afternoon newspaper *La Hora* says: "Agents from the Division of Criminological Investigations commit extrajudicial executions, asserted the Rapporteur for the United Nations."

For almost fifty years Benedicto Tun directed what would perhaps have been the equivalent of this division for the old National Police. Again, I ask myself: Could this have been a "decent" man?—at least in the Orwellian sense? I wonder if I will have a clearer idea about this after my interview with his son.

Saturday morning.

Last night, again, a terrifying nightmare. In the dream, I am at my parents', in the bedroom that we used to call "Grandpa's room." I am awake but lying in bed in the dark. I hear noises and get up to investigate. I walk without turning the lights on, then continue toward the living room and dining room, where the noises are coming from. When I enter, I stop, frightened. A little man, evidently a thief, is leaning on the other side of the table, his back to me; he is searching for something in the cabinet with the glassware. I switch on the lights; the little man turns. He has the face of Mark Rich, a painter (I believe, ultimately, a frustrated one) whom I met in Morocco and who later became a friend in New York but whom I have not heard from in over twenty years. It *is* him! I think—but a lot thinner, and as if in miniature. He seems to be furious, his nose reminiscent of a bat's. I look around me, in search of a blunt object with which to attack him or defend myself. He takes a big flower vase that sits on top of the cabinet where he is snooping around and makes as if to hurl it at me. I let out an inarticulate noise, half scream, half moan, that barely comes out of my mouth. I wake up drenched in sweat. I get up to assure myself that I am all alone in the apartment, then check the main door to make sure it is locked.

I call the chief again. He answers his cell phone and tells me he cannot speak much. He is at the Archive with an "archive guru" who is giving a lecture for the researchers of the Project. The chief sounds very excited. The workshop ends next Monday, and Tuesday there will be a general meeting with the directors and consultants for the Project. He proposes that I start visiting the Archive again on Wednesday morning.

I take a look at *elPeriódico*. More news from Philip Alston: "Rapporteur's findings point to *social cleansing*," states the headline on the front page. Among other statistics, it mentions that, in the year 2006, a total of 5,533 violent deaths were recorded in Guatemala, with only 5 percent of them, approximately, investigated by the authorities, and that sixty-four human rights advocates have been murdered in Guatemala in the last five years.

Another interesting news item:

Jaime Gonzales, the police-doctor, flew from Costa Rica to Venezuela last week on COPA Flight 223, the day after tendering his resignation, and just hours after visiting the police officers detained in connection with the murder of the Salvadoran congressmen at El Boquerón prison—but no record of his arrival at the Simón Bolívar International Airport has been found. In other words: the deputy chief of the National Civil Police has managed to vanish.

Tuesday.

Argument over the phone with B+ (on account of my being late for a date). I tell her she is out of it. She tells me that I do not understand anything. We agree that it is not advisable to talk any further for the time being, and I will call her later. *Old story*, I tell myself.

I have lunch at my parents'. I read in *elPeriódico* an open letter from Jaime Gonzales, where he justifies his departure from Guatemala and his "disappearance." He says: "My death in those circumstances [the scandal surrounding the murder of the Salvadoran congressmen and the execution of their murderers—high-ranking police officers, under Gonzales's command in a high-security Guatemalan prison] would have personally damaged me in the eyes of public opinion." Jesuit logic?

Saturday, Puerto Viejo, Iztapa.

Visiting the T's, overlooking the Chiquimulilla canal. Luxury home, Santa Fe–style, five-star service. But the extreme comfort, along with JL's bonhomie and the company of B+, do not make me completely happy; they don't even put me slightly at ease. (And what about *them*, how do *I* make *them* feel? I could ask myself this question. Have never done it.) Although it is not exactly about "feeling guilty for still having a bit of pure air to breathe [as Adorno used to say] in hell," there is an element of that. Perhaps B+ is right, in what I call her prejudice against the use (however discreet or moderate) of possibly left-linked benzoylmethylecgonine, under the effects of which, and with a slightly trembling hand and a bitter taste in the mouth, I write these lines, stretched out under the blazing sun, by the canal, with the rolling, shimmering sea in the distance.

Sunday afternoon.

In the press: one of the police officers involved in the murder of the Salvadoran congressmen, who is now a protected witness, states that there are "evangelical death squads" composed of National Civil Police agents who belong to various religious sects.

"We are waging," he says, "a battle against Evil. That is how extrajudicial executions are justified."

Monday.

I leaf through my mother's journal telling about her abduction, which I borrowed from her on Thursday. During the six months that she was held captive, my mother was allowed to keep a diary, but they took it away from her when they set her free. A few days after her return home, she started to write down her memories of the events in a hardbound journal, with a fabric cover decorated with very small roses against a bone-colored background. Tucked between the pages of the journal are three sheets of paper typed by my mother (who was a secretary in her youth and an excellent typist until recently). She left the work half-finished, but the first few pages are not without interest:

June 28, 1981. Janila K'ay (her ceramics store).

6:45 p.m. Mario calls to let me know that he will be late for dinner because he has a special meeting at the bank. I take advantage of this to write a note to "Guayito" to order a few items from the factory. At 7:15 Lelo Ungaretti comes by with a message (I do not remember what about) for Mario. I load into the car the defective lamp base to be returned to the factory, along with a wooden fish from Birmania that Rodrigo sent from New York as a gift for Magalí (whose birthday was yesterday), and which I brought to the store to have wrapped. When I get into the car, I see a young man staring at me from across the street, pacing in front of the store. I exit on Seventh Avenue and, as is my habit, I use the access lane on Plazuela España to avoid the red light. I am in a hurry, because I want to have dinner before the 8:00 movie they are going to show on Channel 3. When I turn on to 12th Street, a white van cuts me off. I think it's backing up to park. I see another vehicle in my rearview mirror. Four or five men get out of the van. There is a woman with them. A man I had not seen, and who I imagine got out of the car behind me, breaks the window on the passenger side of my car (I always keep that door locked) with the butt of his gun. I hear gunshots. I scream.

Tuesday.

Long, instructive interview with Benedicto Tun.

The Pasaje Suiza building, which connects 9th and 10th Streets, is today a somber place that still has some of the glamour of the fifties. Tun's office is on the third floor, at the end of the hallway, a hallway that has high wood panels and several waiting benches built into the walls between one office and the next. A Kaqchikel family with two small children and a baby sits on a bench under high windows, with the sunlight filtering in through a film of dust and dirt, eating a snack of black bean soup, avocados, and tortillas. When I walk by them, they offer me lottery tickets. A handwritten note with Tun's cell phone number is stuck to the door of his office. I call him. He tells me he is almost there. I sit on a bench and take notes.

Tun arrives a few minutes late. He has big slanted eyes, a peaceful countenance, and straight salt-and-pepper hair, abundant and well groomed. He makes me think of a slightly overweight, Guatemalan Humphrey Bogart. Through the door that leads to the hallway, there is another door with iron grating. As he gestures to me to go first, he explains that he is remodeling. The office is divided in half with a plywood partition that is missing several panels. He invites me into his office, on the other side of the partition. I sit on a white divan in front of a desk cluttered with papers. I tell him that I assume he has a lot of work and that I do not want to impose on him. He nods with a slight smile of resignation. He goes to his desk and picks up a few old, damaged audiocassettes (which he assumes his father recorded during the last few months of his life), then hands them to me and sits down in an armchair next to the divan. I tell him that before giving them to me, he should listen to the recordings. I remember that I left the tape player in the car. I offer to get it at the end of our interview and loan it to him.

He explains that he found his father's papers to be in a big mess, for which—he confesses—he feels a bit guilty. It seems to me that he is pleased by the interest that I show in the work of his father, of whom he speaks with obvious affection. He shows me a certificate of his father's appointment as chief of the Identification Bureau.

"My father started earning the salary of a simple street agent, but he was serious and ambitious in his scientific pursuit. He was also not dogmatic. He was a practical man, and a scholar who was constantly studying. He created the Identification Bureau practically single-handedly."

I ask him to tell me about the ruling on the death of Castillo Armas, former president of Guatemala, which he had mentioned during our early phone conversations.

Benedicto seems to relax a bit. He starts to tell me in a confidential tone, as if I know the story well, about the case of the soldier Romeo Vásquez, accused of the assassination of President Armas—involving Trujillo, president of the Dominican Republic. He tells me that—as everyone knew from press coverage at the time—this soldier kept a diary. He lets me see photocopies of the diary, with its good, albeit very cramped, handwriting. The notes repeatedly mention the arrival of a "great day" and a "new revolution." Although many have questioned the authenticity of the dairy (including Norman Lewis in his article "Guatemala: The Mystery of the Murdered Dictator"), Tun believes that these circumstances determined Vázquez's fate: to be chosen as the scapegoat by the plotters, likely extreme right-wing people, and not left-wing, as it was claimed at the time. They had masterminded a plot, supposedly an escape plan for the assassin. The soldier was betrayed (the door for his escape from the Presidential Palace was locked from the outside). When he found himself cornered, he shot himself under his chin, with the same rifle he had used to kill the president, according to ballistic tests done by Benedicto Senior. The son shows me photos of the soldier lying on the floor, his head blown apart, with the rifle between his legs.

He starts to talk of another case, the death of Mario Méndez Montenegro. The older Tun pronounced it a suicide (he again talks about the circumstances as if assuming that I know the case well—which flatters me.) "But the people above wanted him to change his pronouncement and say that it had been a homicide," he tells me.

He explains that Méndez Montenegro, presidential candidate and former Police director, killed himself with a revolver. The weapon was a gift from a military man a few years before his death and the bullet that pierced his heart was also of military issue. These facts lent themselves to a hypothesis of political assassination, which was exploited by his supporters. But given the ballistic tests and other circumstances surrounding the death (which took place at his home, after an alcoholic crisis), Tun refused to change his ruling, in spite of the pressures he was subjected to when Mario's brother, Julio César Méndez Montenegro, was elected president of the republic.

"This almost cost him a jail sentence," he assures me. "Given the pressures, he submitted his resignation, but they did not accept it, and he had to continue to work at the Bureau for another three years, until he retired, following an accident."

He comments that his father had an "iron constitution," although at the end he suffered from chronic insomnia.

"He rarely got sick. He used to swim an hour daily, very early, and take cold showers at night or early in the morning," he tells me. He was taking one of those showers when he slipped on a bar of soap and fell to the floor. The impact to his head caused an internal brain hemorrhage, for which he was hospitalized.

He gives me a copy of the resignation letter to read, addressed to the president of the Justice System (as Tun was also the official expert for the courts). I transcribe it below.

Mr. President,

Seeing myself unable to attend to my obligations as Chief of the Identification Bureau of the National Police for over a month, due to a postoperative period following brain trauma that I recently suffered, I consider it my duty to indicate, precisely because the Courts are not completely informed regarding the duties held by subordinate personnel in this Bureau, and due to the fact, since if truth be told, the various obligations related to that position cannot be delegated to a single person, the necessity of a division of labor among the personnel at the Identification Bureau, as follows:

—Examination of fingerprints, palm prints, and footprints found at the crime scene, as well as the identification of cadavers using the post-mortem records.

—Chemical confirmation of gunpowder deflagration, using paraffin gloves.

—Determination of blood stains and other vestiges: sperm, excrement, hair, and various human, animal, or synthetic fibers.

—Analysis of inks and paints, by means of macro and micro-photography, which are indispensable for these studies.

—Analysis of all kinds of handwriting, in every sense, man-uscripts, dactylographic transcripts and authentic or "doubtful" signatures, the study of which is the most requested by the Courts.

—Analysis of photographs.

—Voice analysis.

In addition to "committing himself" to assist the agents or staff members that he recommends to carry out these duties in certain cases, he awaits the attention and response of the president of the Judicial Body.

I tell Benedicto that I do not want to take any more of his time—it is now past noon—and we agree to another interview after Easter, upon my return from my trip to France.

He assures me that over the holidays he will have time to continue to review his father's documents, and he promises to set aside those that he thinks might interest me. We get up and Benedicto goes to open the grate door that leads to the hallway, which he keeps locked—he explains again—"for peace of mind."

Down below, at the end of the hallway and outlined against the glare of the sun coming in from the street, the silhouette of a police pickup truck can be seen. I have a bad feeling when I see two agents get out of it. They stare at me as they approach me, but they do not detain me.

I go for the tape player in the car, which I left in a public parking lot, and return to Tun's office to give it to him.

Afternoon.

I read *Prensa Libre* until it's time to pick up Pía to sleep over at my apartment: yesterday the president of the republic accepted the resignations of the minister of the Interior and the director of the National Police, following the scandal related to the Salvadoran congressmen. Adela de Torrebiarte, the newly appointed minister, belonged to the Anguished Mothers and, later, the President's Security Advisory Council, and was also friends with my parents.

I call JL to talk about the trip I want to make to Río Dulce with Pía and my mother, in a small plane belonging to their construction company. In passing, I make some comments about what Benedicto told me regarding the death of Méndez

Montenegro, who was JL's relative. Then—and this surprises me a bit—JL tells me that he has a long-distance phone call and needs to hang up, but that he will call me later. He does not call back.

Nighttime.

Pía is asleep. I speak again with JL. I allude to our conversation from this afternoon. He tells me he does not want to talk about "that" over the phone—causing me to see that I have not been very discreet. I believe he is overreacting, but I say nothing about it, and we change the topic of our conversation.

Wednesday morning.

Chaotic violin concerto by Pía and her school friends. I had agreed to go to the Archive after the show. I call the chief to confirm my visit, the first since the "suspension." He tells me a new difficulty has arisen and that he will have to be present to ensure that I will be allowed into the Archive. He will call me—he says—a bit later on my cell.

Afternoon.

No news from the chief. I call him. He answers. He apologizes for the cancellation and explains that more problems have come up. He does not want me to return to the Archive without us speaking first—in person, he insists, not over the phone. He gives me an appointment for tomorrow at five in the afternoon at the usual café, next to the Taco Bell on Avenida de las Américas.

Early in the evening, I visit my parents—I bring some therapeutic icepacks for my mother, who has a sore knee. I keep them company while they have supper (they eat very early, around seven). I describe my interview with Tun in broad strokes.

"You're playing with fire," my father says.

I respond that I do not think it is that big of a deal, that a lot of time has elapsed (since the Castillo Armas case, for example).

My mother remains silent. It's an indulgent silence.

Thursday, early evening.

The chief arrived twenty minutes late to our five o'clock appointment, but he was extraordinarily cordial—almost apologetic—about his delay. "Traffic," he said. "I haven't had lunch yet."

While he gobbled down a burrito, he remembered that in a futuristic movie he recently saw, the Taco Bell logo appears at a restaurant where they serve tacos and other snacks made of human flesh. He did not have good news for me. There have been a series of issues, "work-related in particular," at the Archive Recovery Project. Some have been caused by my presence there. At the general meeting they just had (at La Bodeguita on 12th Street), he explained, there was "a sea of long faces" among the Project directors and workers for granting me, not a part of the Project, the privilege of visiting the Archive.

I reply that I am not surprised at all and that I expected something like this, since other people's privileges tend to cause discomfort.

"As a matter of fact, I do not really need to go back," I tell him, "although I would like to."

He assures me that I will be able to go back; he just does not know when.

I ask if I could have access to some documents that I had started to look at: the Police Yearly Reports, which have already been digitized and are public documents, in fact.

That could be a problem, he says; he would have to provide explanations in order to obtain that material. However, he promises to loan me the Yearly Report from the Archive Recovery Project to read, which he himself created, and which could be useful as a source for the book I may write.

A bit surprised, I tell him that I would like to take that report with me on my next trip to France. We agree that he will give me a CD with that text in a few days.

"Take good care," he tells me as we say goodbye with a strong handshake in the parking lot.

Tuesday afternoon.

The chief calls. He tells me that he is revising the text for his Yearly Report, that he has found some errors he wants to correct, and that he will not be able to do it for another three or four days. So, we agree that I will stop by the Archive upon my return from Río Dulce, on Holy Wednesday (and before dropping Pía off at her cousins' in a condominium on the Pacific coast, where Pia's mother Isabel will be spending Easter Week).

By chance, I find the photocopies of the article by Marta Elena Casaús, in which she talks about Fernando Juárez Muñoz, a contemporary of Miguel Ángel Asturias who, influenced by theosophy and by authors such as Madame Blavatski, Annie Besant, and Jiddu Krishnamurti, maintained that the Maya did not belong to an inferior race and forecast, back in 1922, that in order *to form a true positive nation, it would be essential for the indigenous people to fully incorporate into the citizenry with the same rights and duties as any other Guatemalans, and that their cultural richness should be recognized. . . .* Of course, Miguel Ángel & Co. did not agree. At that time, the future Nobel laureate wrote: *Truth be told, the Indian shows signs of psychological degeneration; he is a fanatic, a drug addict, and cruel.* Or: *Let us do with the Indian as with other animal species, such as cattle, when they present symptoms of degeneration.*

Holy Saturday, before dawn.

New quarrel with B+ after dinner last night. In reality—I believe—she is upset over my upcoming trip to France. She complains about my lack of empathy, my problem with "feelings I cannot handle." It is clear, I think: what cannot be handled is usually problematic.

JL's pilot calls to tell me that we will leave with a delay of three hours.

Ten in the morning.

We are leaving for Río Dulce in one hour. Magalí, who I spoke with a moment ago, warns me that Luisa is accompanying my mother. "It is the first time the poor thing will fly. If I were you, I'd have plastic bags handy in case she needs to throw up." Clear skies.

La Buga, Río Dulce, afternoon.

I read in W. H. Auden (*The Dyers Hand*): "The unacknowledged legislators of the world: the secret police."

I think again about the young female archivist who told me about the action radiograms a few hours before my "suspension." When they asked me her name I said I did not know, which was true. I regret not memorizing it when we introduced ourselves. As much as I try, I am unable to remember.

From the east bank of the river, snippets of music drift over the deep, dark canyon of oleaginous water: evangelical songs, hymns bastardized with Mexican *corridos* and American spirituals.

I start reading *Paseo eterno*. It is, I think, the best book by Javier Mejía, but at the same time it is the worst. The best because he has removed the mask and he talks and writes just like he thinks; the worst because, as always, or perhaps here more than ever, he takes too much pleasure in his own version of himself. A crude criticism, perhaps, but I say it with an unexpected enthusiasm and with the certainty that if he stopped looking at himself with that odd and inexplicable self-complacency, he might become an interesting writer.

Time makes people change their minds—Voltaire.

Sartre, in *Nausea*: "I believe that is the risk of keeping a diary: you exaggerate everything, you have expectations, and you exceed the limits of truth."

Wittgenstein: "But is this not the unilateral consideration of tragedy that it only shows that an encounter can determine our entire life?"

Schnitzler: "Every truth has its moment—its revelation— which tends to be short, such that, like existence itself, it is the glow, or just a spark, between nothing or between the lie that precedes it and the one that follows, between the moment that seems paradoxical and the moment that begins to seem trivial."

Wednesday.

Upon returning from Río Dulce, this time by land (my mother's chauffeur came to pick us up), we stop by La Isla, which is at the beginning of the highway that links the capital with the Atlantic coast, to pick up the CD with the Yearly Report from the Archive Recovery Project that the chief said he would leave for me with one of the guards. This way I will avoid crossing the city from one end to the other twice tomorrow.

It is almost nighttime when we arrive at La Isla, and in order to get to the Archive we have to go through two security checkpoints. Armed guards are everywhere. My mother, whom I had not sufficiently warned about these circumstances, looks at me with alarm, and I think she is impressed when they let us in after I talk to the guards. Further down, at the gate to the Archive, the guard on duty, after confirming my identity, hands me an envelope with the CD promised by the chief, and, in addition, a small cardboard box with four CDs, on which I read in longhand: *National Police Yearly Report*. I seem to recognize Luis Galíndez's handwriting from the envelope he gave me with the elimination list from the military archives.

"This is also for you," the guard tells me.

As we leave:

"Do you work here?" Pía asks.

I laugh, and say sometimes.

"Are you a policeman?"

"No."

"So then?"

106

"I investigate *them*," I answer and laugh again.

"Why?" Pía insists.

"It's part of my job."

"You investigate them?"

After thinking about it for a moment, I improvise:

"I want to make sure they are behaving."

Pía stops asking. Out of the corner of my eye I see my mother, who stares at the darkness outside the car, smiling faintly in silence.

Fourth Sketchbook: Leather Cover, No Branding, No Name

Easter Sunday, in Paris, chez Miquel Barceló.

I leaf through, among Miquel's books, *The People's Act of Love* by James Meek. I find the description of a character that, I think, would fit JL—that is, JL as a type is clearly recognizable: *He was an architect and builder, one of those charmed individuals whose practical usefulness transcends any amount of snobbery, corruption, and stupidity in the powers on whose patronage they depend.*

Since October of last year, when I was visiting here, Miquel has acquired several dozen books. This growth rate is normal for his vast library. Almost all the new books seem to have been used, possibly read.

Tomorrow I'm going to Poitiers to deliver the lecture I prepared on Good Friday in Amatitlán: "Landscape and Biography."

Monday at noon in Paris.

Last night I dreamed of Pía. She called me on the phone (in the dream, I was in the chalet in Amatitlán where I spent a few days with B+). Pía makes me talk with her maternal grandfather, Don Carlos, a fighter-plane and crop-duster pilot. Jovial conversation. He tells me that he is going to pick me up and, with the speed of dreams, suddenly he is there, in the garden of the chalet, standing next to his sports car (which he actually does not have). He drives me at high speed back to the capital. He drives recklessly, I ride scared. (In my dream I think: he is a fighter pilot, he masters the car.) We stop near a village that could be Villa Canales, where a fair is taking place. There are rides and water games with Maya themes. Great fun. We engage—or rather, I engage, because at a certain moment Don Carlos disappears from the dream—in hand-to-hand combat and war maneuvers, with a background of inflatable plastic pyramids. Childish euphoria.

Last night I had dinner with Claude Thomas, who translated Paul and Jane Bowles into French, near her home in Montmartre. I tell her about the Archive, about the diary I am keeping. She listens with interest. What I tell her has the elements of a thriller, she tells me. Later she asks me if I miss Paul. I assure her that I do. In a simplified version I tell her about my recurring dream about Paul: I go back to Tangier and I find him alive, although very old and sick, in his old apartment in the Itesa building. The apartment is empty, without a single book. I ask him if he does not need his books (which I sold a few years back to Miquel), and Paul says that yes, he would like to have them back. I promise him that I will give them back to him, and then I awake, anguished.

"You must feel guilty," Claude tells me.

I ask her why I should feel guilty. She does not answer, and we start talking about something else.

Wednesday in Poitiers. Early morning. Insomnia.

A rush of memories from the conversation, more or less alcohol-soaked, with Homero Jaramillo, who came from Montreal for the colloquium on Central American literature. I tell him what I've been doing at the Archive, and I tell him about my fear that among those who work there, there might be some who were involved in the kidnapping of my mother. (He was the "political liaison" in Mexico for a Salvadoran guerrilla movement, and there he established links with

Guatemalan guerrillas. It was he who, about ten years ago, introduced me to the person who claimed that my mother had been kidnapped by an urban guerrilla commando.)

Homero mentions the possibility of earning a scholarship at the University of Toronto. I tell him that perhaps I would be interested. He nods, saying nothing more about it.

Thursday, chez Miquel.

Homero, who was invited to dinner last night at Miquel's, does not show up. I call him on the phone. He apologizes. He is a bit drunk and very tired, he tells me. He is staying for dinner at the house of Colombian friends who are hosting him, who have lived in Paris for some time. With Miquel, I talk again about the Archive. He tells me that he also assumed, when he heard that I was doing "research" there, that one of my motives would be to find out something about the kidnapping of my mother. I tell him that is not the case, but that of course I would like to learn as much as possible about that.

"Sure," he says, "but you should clarify for the 'chief' that you will not use what you find for legal or judicial purposes—right?"

I tell him that I don't know if they would believe me.

"Yes," he answers. "You're right, they're not going to believe you."

Phone call from Lucca, the small town in Tuscany where my sister Mónica settled a few months ago with her four children. She invites me to go visit them. A little later, a call from my mother in Guatemala: she insists that I go to Italy, and she offers to pay for my plane ticket to prevent me from using my wallet as a pretext not to go.

I am pleased to think that Mónica and her children are far

away from Guatemala. Safe, I think. I cannot stop imagining that perhaps in the not-too-distant future I will go into exile again. And of course I worry how something like that could affect Pía's future.

Friday. Five in the morning. Sleepless.

I had dinner last night with Alice Audouin, whom I had not seen for years. I talked to her about the Archive. She asked if working on something like that didn't put me in physical danger. I answered—with a bit of exaggeration—that in a country like Guatemala everyone lives in constant physical danger. Alice said: "Ah, the danger, the dignity of danger, here we have lost it."

I got back to Miquel's house around midnight. I called B+ several times, both her home and her cell phones. She does not answer. In Guatemala it would be four in the afternoon.

Saturday.

I read *Balzac*, the short biography by Zweig. He says this about some manuscripts by Balzac: "One can see how the lines, which at first are neat and orderly, then swell up like the veins of an angry man." Something similar could be seen in my writing, I think.

About Fouché, Napoleon's minister of police, of whom Zweig also speaks in the work about Balzac: "He needed intrigue as much as nourishment."

Lunch with Guillermo Escalón, the cameraman. It's the birthday of his son Sebastián, who is thinking of going to live in Guatemala for a while.

"Why?" I ask him.

"I'm fed up with Paris," he says. And also fed up with the

magazine (by France's National Scientific Research Center), where he has been working as a reporter for a few years).

I eat dinner alone at the Pick-Clops, near Miquel's studio.

Then a very late, amorous call from B+. Alluding to a comment of mine about her habit of scolding me, she recites these verses by her beloved Sor Juana: *Listen to me, if you can, with your eyes . . . / since my rough voice does not reach you, / hear me, deaf one, as I complain in silence.*

"But I cannot see you," I say.

"That does not matter, silly." she answers. "It is not about that; you can see me in your imagination, no?"

I ask her what she is wearing.

Sunday.

First night of normal sleep since I arrived in Europe a week ago. A beautiful sunny day. Appointment with Claude to have lunch in Montmartre.

Vague memory of a dream with Roberto Lemus, who works in the Archive and is one of the possible kidnappers of my mother. He is a pallid man, medium height, with drooping shoulders, a round belly, and a certain intellectual air, which, in the dream, makes me think of Allen Ginsberg. He has light green eyes and big jug ears. He reads a newspaper aloud. He has a nasal, phlegmatic voice. (I must listen to the cassettes we recorded during the kidnapping negotiations; that voice could be the voice of the negotiator, I think when I wake up.)

Mónica calls me again on the phone. I confirm my travel plans to Italy next week. She will pick me up at Pisa airport with the landlady of the apartment where she lives.

Difficult viewing and reading, on my laptop, of the CDs

with the *National Police Yearly Reports* that I have brought with me. Thus far, I have not been able to find the reports on the Identification Bureau prepared by Benedicto Tun. Surprise. On the cover of the Yearly Report from 1964, instead of the usual plain cover with no art, a small graphic discovery: a representation in perspective, with a single vanishing point, of a large, open tome. On the bottom edge of the tome, police handcuffs. Above the book, looming over it, a bat with outstretched wings. The caption, "Yearly Report," in Gothic characters. The effect is sinister.

I show it to Miquel and notice with satisfaction his slight startled jump.

"Man, that is even a little bit scary." He leans toward the screen. "That bat was lovingly made."

"Yes. There are those who love their job," I say.

Monday.

Before getting out of bed, I read the *Stendhal* by Zweig.

Another splendid day, with a little less heat than yesterday.

A revelation in the shower: it's not so much that I am bothered by the erudition of others—Miquel's, Guillermo's, or Homero's—in their different "fields of knowledge," as much as by the awareness of the immensity of my own overall ignorance, the horizons of which, as I acquire new knowledge, or glimpses of knowledge, seem wider each day.

Tuesday.

When I open my eyes, "the dregs of my dreams are lost." At night, while I tossed and turned in bed unable to fall asleep, my thoughts went to the CDs from the Archive, which I believe came into my hands thanks to Galíndez. I have found copies of several files after 1970, which I am not supposed to see. When I showed Miquel the image of the bat, I mentioned this.

"Those documents," I said. "I prefer to not even open them."

"But why not?" he replies. "Maybe they gave them to you because they want you to see them."

I have dinner with Gustavo Guerrero, the editor at Gallimard. He proposes that I write something for the *Nouvelle Revue Française* about *Borges* by Bioy, which I consider to be a secretly complex, unique, magnificent book. This, following our conversation about an article that came out a few days ago in *El Mundo*, where Bioy's integrity and that of the editors of the book is questioned: "Let us remember," the article says, "that Bioy never wanted to publish those diaries, and they are being published by others, who may or may not have manipulated the writer's private mischief."

I dream about a traffic violation. By mistake, I drive in the wrong direction in front of the barracks of the Fortress of the Honor Guard, on Avenida de la Reforma. Two soldiers standing at the door aim at me with old rifles. I fear they might shoot, but they allow me to turn around and drive away.

Wednesday.

Last night I dined with Marcos Cisneros, the Colombian editor and Homero's friend. It seems to me that he has not yet read *Borges* by Bioy, although during our telephone conversation that afternoon he told me that to him it seemed "an excellent book."

I return late, quite drunk. I call B+ several times; I do not find her.

I wake up out of sorts. I can't remember any dreams.

At noon, Miquel tells me about the bronze elephant, part of his exhibition opening next Saturday. It is a young elephant with its legs up in the air, balanced on the tip of its trunk. It's a "comical" piece, about four meters high and weighing about fifteen hundred kilos.

At the last minute, Miquel's Paris dealer, Yvon Lambert, does not want to exhibit it in his gallery, out of fear that the floor may not be able to bear so much weight. Furthermore, the insurer refuses to cover the risks. Miquel decides to go to the gallery, to propose a solution. I go with him.

YL welcomes Miquel into his office and greets him effusively. However, during the visit Miquel spends his time insulting YL, without YL ever taking the hint.

"This used to be a nice gallery," Miquel tells YL, "but it seems that each year it gets smaller. Have you moved the partitions?"

YL acknowledges that he has reduced the space of the main showroom in order to add another room. To change the subject, YL asks Miquel about one of his female friends, who used to live in Paris and now lives in Spain.

"What?" Miquel says to him. "You're into girls now?"

YL's assistant shows Miquel a copy of the catalog for his exhibition, which she just received from the printer. The color reproduction leaves something to be desired. But Miquel focuses on the new gallery logo, which appears on the cover.

"It's okay," he says. "It reminds me of the shirt designer's logo."

And so on, until we say goodbye—and by then YL's mood no longer seems as good as it did at the beginning.

In the afternoon, travel to Italy.

Thursday. In Lucca.

They come to pick me up at the airport, which is about forty minutes from Lucca: Mónica and the Luccan couple—Mr. Rino and Mrs. Angela—who rent her the apartment where she has settled with her children. They are an older couple. As we leave the parking garage, Mr. Rino, who drives a compact Mercedes, has difficulty paying the electronic ticket, and says to his wife: "Ma cosa vuoi? Sono un vecchietto."

We get lost on the way. We stop to ask for directions in a cozy restaurant, so we decide to have dinner there. It is nine thirty at night. At dinner I learn that Mr. Rino, sixty-six, is retired. He was a tailor. Angela, his wife, treats Mónica with great affection. It seems to me that she has extended her vocation as an Italian mother—she has a daughter already married and no longer living there.

They both evince enormous ignorance about the world in general, an ignorance similar to that which I encountered about fifteen years ago in our Italian relatives from Piedmont—great-uncles, cousins twice removed. When they hear Mónica and me speak Spanish, Mr. Rino expresses amazement. "La vostra lingua è veramente una lingua latina," he says.

I explain that "Guatemalan" is, except for the accent and some regionalisms, the same language as Spanish.

"But you," he says, "are not Spanish. The Spaniards killed so many Indians and committed so many atrocities."

"Yes," I say. "And they brought the Spanish language to America. We are the heirs to those Spaniards, at least in part.

"Is that so?" he exclaims, a little surprised.

"It is clear," I say, "that we [I look at Mónica, to indicate her as an example] are not Maya, okay? We have some Maya in us, but our names are European, and we have Italian blood on our father's side. But we are also descendants of the conquistadors. We are also the bad guys!" I laugh.

Mrs. Angela and Mr. Rino seem dismayed.

We arrive in Lucca at midnight. Mónica's apartment is small but comfortable. The children seem happy. The two older ones have received scholarships for higher education, and they have already been offered jobs. The little ones learn Italian.

In the morning I discover, outside the window in the dining room, a nice view over a large medieval garden with big trees, where yellow-legged birds flutter above the dark foliage.

Friday.

Last night, I had a cocaine dream, with Carter Coleman, Bret Easton Ellis, Alejandro D—my old friend from Cobán—and JL. A clear substance that, upon making contact with the palm of my hand, turns into small ice cubes. Banal conversation with Alejandro (about something that happened in Cobán). He seemed a bit conflicted. He said that he no longer wants the drug and yet takes it in large quantities.

After lunch, on a stroll along the walls surrounding Lucca, I speak with Mauro, Mónica's eldest son, about Guatemala. Mauro is interested in knowing how things are over there. I tell him about the Salvadoran congressmen assassinated by policemen, then we talk about the scandal at the Ministry of Education (over the illicit transfer of funds to the Ministry of Public Works for the construction of a new airport), and about Rigoberta Menchú's presidential run. Mauro asks a series of questions about how a country like Guatemala could change for the better. We come to the conclusion that, miracles aside, there's nothing good to be expected, except perhaps a moral revolution (unlikely) or intervention by a higher power.

"Like that of the United States in Iraq?" Mauro asks, and we laugh.

I tell him that things are going to get worse long before they get better. I tell him that maybe the thing is not to think about how to change things, but how to get away from it all. That his destiny is not necessarily there, that maybe he should consider the possibility of living in another country.

"I would like to return," he answers.

"Why not study political science?" I ask, not without irony.

He shakes his head doubtfully, and does not answer.

I talk to him about Haiti, "practically converted into a cemetery," as a Spanish columnist recently said.

"Guatemala could end up that way too, if things do not change," I say.

Mauro could very well have asked why I went back to Guatemala, which would be difficult to explain, but he did not ask.

That afternoon I travel back to Paris.

Saturday, chez Miquel in Paris.

Joubert, quoted by Du Bos: *La bonhomie est une perfection*.

Homero, who had agreed to call me last night to have dinner together (he goes back to Montreal tomorrow morning) does not call.

Late at night at Miquel's, with his daughter Marcela, we watch *Short Cuts* by Altman.

Sunday.

Miquel's exhibit, yesterday afternoon, a success.

The young bronze elephant is on display in a cobbled

courtyard, in a private small palace belonging to a friend of Miquel's, very close to YL's gallery. People exclaim and smile when they see it, balanced on its straight trunk with its legs extended into the air and its little tail pointing up toward the sky. In the gallery, a display of large canvases with enormous skulls surrounded by burnt matches, open shells, and snails drying in the sun—still lifes, *memento mori* and *vanitas*, that simultaneously evoke the tradition whence they come while merrily distancing themselves from it.

In the evening, dinner at Maxim's. I talk for a while with Castor Siebel, octogenarian art critic, an old friend of Miquel's. I am surprised by his good memory; he remembers my full name, and the only time that we met before, about ten years ago, with Miquel, in a brasserie. He asks me where I live now. "Don't you feel threatened," he asks later, "living in Guatemala?" I tell him that saying yes would be an exaggeration but saying no would not be the exact truth.

On a recommendation from Miquel, I read the first chapters of Zweig's *Fouché*, "inventor of the political police," and often cited by Tun in the Yearly Reports.

In the afternoon, in his studio, Miquel shows me the experiments he is working on with materials and paint for his project for the dome of the Palace of Nations, home of the United Nations Office in Geneva. It is a seascape with a surface area of about one thousand square meters. "The dome is huge," he says, "like a bullring, but upside down." He also shows me pieces for a stage set that he might soon create for Peter Brook. They are something like large pillows made with balls of newspaper pasted with a little diluted glue onto undulating sheets. Viewed from the side, they are reminiscent of the cross section of flat, striated muscle fiber of a cactus leaf.

"This," he tells me, "could be used to make beds and other

furniture, and perhaps even homes for poor people." I think of teaching the technique to Pía after returning to Guatemala.

Almost at dawn, back from the party at Maxim's, I call B+. She scolds me when she realizes what time it is in Paris, and that I'm "too cheerful." I tell her she is exaggerating. In the end, we agree that she will pick me up at the airport on Tuesday. The flight, I tell her, will arrive almost at midnight. She complains about the late hour but assures me that she will be there.

I read De Quincey, *Essays on Style, Rhetoric, and Language*, and through him I come to Salvator Rosa, the "bandit painter and satirical author from the seventeenth century" (possibly our ancestor?) beloved by the English romantics, who wrote:

"Our wealth must be spiritual, and we must content ourselves with small sips while others choke on prosperity."

Monday.

Last night, with Miquel, we saw *Notes from the Underground*, a curious and interesting adaptation of Dostoyevsky's story transplanted to Los Angeles. We spoke once again of the expedition project to El Golea (Algeria), to look for the blockhouse with the frescoes by François Augiéras.

I have a dream about an experiment with "Barceló blocks." In the dream, Pía and I build a great pyramid in a vacant lot in Guatemala City, where I return tomorrow.

Tuesday. Seven thirty in the morning (before leaving for the airport).

Yesterday, Guillermo Escalón took me to visit Jacobo Rodríguez Padilla, a Guatemalan artist who is eighty-five, exiled in Paris since the fifties, shortly after the overthrow of Arbenz and the Revolutionary Government. Tiny studio apartment: the antithesis, one could say, of Miquel's studio. He has some very curious canvases, part surrealist and part naïve. A vague palette that allows for all colors. He showed us several very small sculptures that I liked a lot, especially one made of alabaster that made me think of an ancient Chinese work. The artist is small, very thin, and seems exceedingly fragile, like a little bird, one could say. He told me that Guillermo has told him about the project at the Archive that I have been working on. Jacobo asked several questions. I told him about the Identification Bureau. He immediately mentioned Benedicto Tun.

"Could he have been related to Francisco Tun, the painter, or not?" he asked in jest, and then, he added, in seriousness: "That man was feared. He knew a lot. He was considered a technician or a scientist more than a policeman. But we were not sure it was advisable to keep such a person at his post, after the Revolution. In any case, he stayed there."

Later, after leaving the studio, while we walked towards Le Prosper, Guillermo told me that Jacobo's sister was killed by the Guatemalan army.

"He has not managed to shake off his guilt over this," he explained. "He once told me: 'Imagine. I got her into all that. I led her to the party, and just a month later they captured her.'"

Guillermo went on to tell me that the young woman had four or five children, and that her husband, who had also gone into exile in Paris, committed suicide shortly after.

"He was crazy," Guillermo said. "You know how he killed himself? He threw himself off the top of a cardboard replica of Mount Everest at a zoo on the outskirts of Paris. Can you believe it?"

Wednesday morning, in Guatemala.

B+ comes to pick me up at the airport, she stays over. All is well.

I listen to the messages on the answering machine. Calls from the bank, due to activity on my credit card and some deposit from a literary agency. Another call from Lucía Morán, whom I think I neglected to tell I was going to be traveling. And another from a company that offers funeral services at home.

Afternoon.

I pick Pía up from school at noon. While I wait for the violin lesson to finish, her teacher—who months ago had asked me to come and tell a story or a fable to the class—tells me that she is very worried because she believes that for some time now she has been watched. The teacher, a lady in her fifties, is a redhead with a voluptuous shape, a bit extravagant and no doubt attractive for her age.

"There is something angelic about her," says the father of another one of the girls in her class, and I have to agree. She is naturally sweet, although somewhat nervous, and she has the curious tic of covering her mouth with one hand when she speaks.

"Two guys sit in their parked car in front of my house almost every morning. When I look at them, they look away and do whatever, like play with their cell phones or look at a newspaper or a magazine. Now I have to change my route every day to come to school, to the extent that's possible, of course," she says, with her nervous laugh.

I tell her that I think she is doing the right thing (even if her followers are imaginary).

Thursday.

Very hot night, and dreamless.

I call Benedicto Tun in the morning. He tells me that he has gathered more material about his father. I agree to call him next Wednesday to arrange another interview.

I call the chief at the Archive Recovery Project. A woman answers his cell phone; she tells me that he is traveling and won't be back until Saturday.

Lunch at Magalí's house; her daughter Alani celebrates her seventeenth birthday. I tell María Marta and Alejandra, Magalí's youngest daughter, about the call I got from the funeral company. María Marta says, as if to minimize any implied threat, that she got a call several days back with the same offer.

"Well," I answer, "then I'm letting myself be carried away by my imagination. Perhaps it was not a threat."

"Maybe," says Alejandra. "Or maybe they want to threaten both of you, or the entire family. Me, on the other hand, not having the same last name, not even funeral homes call me, and no one bothers to threaten me. Very sad, my case," she laughs.

Friday.

Yesterday, after returning to the apartment with Pía from the supermarket where we'd been to shop for the weekend, it occurred to me to call back the number of the supposed funeral home while she was amusing herself with the little dresses, books, and jigsaw puzzles that I brought her from Paris. There was no answer.

A bit later, the phone rang and I answered. At first, I heard nothing. Then, there was a giggle like that of an old lady,

126

which I can only describe as evil. The number, "unknown." Suddenly, I felt an attack of nausea, and I ran to the bathroom. Pía, who came behind me, was scared to see me, arched as I was over the toilet bowl, vomiting.

"What's wrong with you?" she asked, on the verge of tears.

I told her that maybe something I ate at lunch did not sit well with me.

I felt very weak. I lay down for a moment on the makeshift sofa in the living room. Then I got up to give Pía some cereal, and I had some yogurt. We got into bed and fell asleep immediately.

Today I woke up with a fever, with pain all over my body. I called Pía's maternal grandmother (her mother is traveling). I explained that I am sick, that I will not be able to take Pía to school. The grandmother came to pick her up a bit later. At noon, B+ brings me fever reducers, pain killers, and several bottles of water.

I must find out whose number I called yesterday afternoon, although I suppose it could be a public telephone.

Saturday.

Reading *Fouché*. In the afternoon, already without discomfort and without a fever, I go to pick up Pía at her grandmother's, then we go to visit my parents. At night, mild abdominal and back pain.

Incredible period, ominous and homicidal, when the Universe is transformed into a dangerous place.—Zweig.

I think about how to use "Barceló blocks" to build a refuge-labyrinth that could also serve as an allegory.

Sunday.

I wake up at six. Uneasy. Dissatisfied. I'm cured.

It's a gray morning. The cries and calls of birds can be heard, as always, drifting up from the ravine below the window in my room.

Last night I brought a stack of newspapers from my parents' home to go through the news for the days when I was away. Sad pastime. But, what other country could I live in now? I ask myself. I think of the bourgeois condemned at the time of Fouché to "the dry guillotine," as they called exile in places like Guyana—or Guatemala? But the idea of emigrating yet again—to the United States? Europe? Mexico? Argentina? or even Africa?—does not seem reasonable to me, at least not yet. That is to say, I do not feel sufficiently threatened to flee. Meanwhile, I keep looking at the news.

I have the idea that, instead of throwing away the newspapers, I can use them to make "Barceló blocks" with Pía for construction projects. Who knows, maybe that way we'll find a path, an exit, or at least a lasting distraction: building houses for the poor, or dollhouses, pyramids or walls, labyrinths of bulky, fluffy newspaper blocks.

Afternoon.

Late in the morning a cool, dry northern wind began to blow. The weather has changed now, and it is placid, with a sky as blue as a day in December.

Instead of going to El Tular like I do almost every Sunday, I ask Magalí for permission to experiment with the paper blocks in her yard. At Magalí's house, two men from Petén, Danilo Dubón and his assistant César, are repairing the thatched roof that the winter winds have damaged. Danilo, whom I met in Petexbatún several years ago, is a woodworker and builder of extraordinary integrity and taste. He has emigrated to the capital in search of employment as a master builder, and in one year he has become quite prosperous; he just bought land on the outskirts of the city and is starting to build his home.

While he and César replace the damaged thatched roof on the house, Pía helps me crumple pages of old newspapers—though she saves some of them, those she wants to keep because of a picture of a baby or a pet—and I glue them together in alternate rows on the spread-out sheets. In a few minutes we use up three or four newspapers and we have the first block, similar to the ones I saw in Miquel's studio in Paris, so I consider the experiment a success.

At the end of the morning, I show the blocks that we have made to Danilo and César, submitting them to their judgment as builders. When they see them, they laugh. Danilo tries to compress a block with his hands, and the block resists. They now seem to grasp the possibilities.

"And that paper," César tells me, "you can get everywhere."

"It could work," says Danilo. "Maybe with a little varnish on top, in case of rain, or fire."

Fifth Sketchbook: Spanish Binding

Something that is also saddening is doing things that one knows will leave no memory.

BORGES, quoted by BIOY

A few days ago, I learned something that still amuses me. They have a nickname for me at the Archive: "El Matrix." I have to admit that I feel like *un'oca in un clima d'aquile* in that place. Is it possible that my discoveries there were directed, that is, *foreseen*? I wonder sometimes. "They let you see only what they want you to see, right?" B+ said to me one day. "So, what do you expect?" As in a Kafka parable, to enter the dusty labyrinth that is the Archive at La Isla, all I had to do was to ask permission. Inside: dark, damp room after dark, damp room, piled high with papers that have a patina of rat and bat droppings, teeming with more than a hundred anonymous heroes, in their lab coat uniforms, protected by masks and latex gloves, and surveilled by policemen, concentric circles of policemen, policemen who belonged to the same repressive forces whose crimes the archivists investigate.

Monday.

Long and anguished dream about a police pursuit. I'm the one being pursued. The hunt is directed by a character whom I guess my subconscious created, inspired by the elder Tun. I do not know why they look for me. They have given me a reprieve, a window of time to leave the country, and that window is about to close. I consult with several people—my father, Gonzalo Marroquín, and a lawyer of dubious reputation. They all advise me to leave. I think of Pía. I do not want to be away from her, I say. "But," Gonzalo replies, "you don't want her to have to visit you in jail." He mentions several people we both know who have gone to jail in recent days. They have been captured under Tun's orders, he explains, and despite being influential people it seems that it will not be easy for them to regain their freedom. I think about hiding, but I have little time to find the ideal hiding place. Suddenly, I am running upstairs in a circular house with a conical roof that looks a lot like the Petexbatún house—magnificent woodwork, very high thatched roof—except that this one has several floors and rooms and is very tangled. Some policemen look for me on the lower floor. I am already hidden near the thatched apex. The policemen give up and go back out. I don't dare to move, although I'm in an impossible position, and my back and neck hurt. After a silence that seems very long, I hear people outside. I recognize my mother's voice. She is speaking with other women. I come down from my hiding place with difficulty. I get out of the house. The women, I realize, are a group of Anguished Mothers. They tell me that I have to leave the place, that they will still look for me. I cannot remain in the country. The dream, which I remember fuzzily after that moment, continues, winding through roads that cross mountains, gorges, and ravines. I realize that I'm going to Belize, and I think about how much time will pass before I see Pía again.

Tuesday, May 1.
I finish reading *Fouché* by Zweig.
The idea of offering my "services" to the new minister of the Interior crosses my mind unexpectedly.

Wednesday.
Dreamless night.

Yesterday, excursion to El Tular with Pía. We made more "Barceló blocks." I told Pía that we are going to make a dollhouse with these blocks. "A house I'll fit into?" she asked me. I assured her that she will. In the afternoon we went horseback riding through the old forest and we swam in the pool.

I did not see B+ yesterday; another small argument. She sent me a text message around six o'clock in the morning to complain about what she calls "my horrible pride."

Intense lower back pain.

I read Voltaire's *Memoirs*, which I had barely thumbed through in Paris. In the first few pages, he writes about how King Frederick William of Prussia wanted (but was not able) to have his son and heir, Frederick, beheaded for wanting to leave the kingdom to travel the world. *It seems*—says Voltaire by way of conclusion—*that neither divine laws nor human laws clearly express that a young man should be beheaded for having had the desire to travel.*

Quarter past ten.

I call Benedicto Tun. We make an appointment for tomorrow at ten in his office. He has, he says, two important rulings that his father made, and he wants to show them to me. I tell him that, during my previous visit, I saw that next to his office was the office of Arturo Rodríguez, a leftist military official who led an attempted coup against another military man, General Miguel Ydígoras Fuentes, under whose government the first great repressive wave of the sixties began. I ask him if his father and Rodríguez were friends. He says no, but that he is friendly with Rodríguez and that, if I want, he can introduce me later. He carefully takes a picture out of a drawer to show me: it's from the christening of Miguel Ángel Asturias, eldest son of Rodrigo, future head of the Organization of the People in Arms (ORPA) and the Guatemalan Revolutionary Union (URNG). He was baptized by Monsignor Rossell y Arellano, who, a few years later, would be archbishop of Guatemala. The godfather is none other than Ydígoras Fuentes. I ask him where he got it. He says he found it among the papers from his father.

I call the chief; he is in a meeting, he tells me, and he will call me later.

Thursday.
Last night, heavy drinking.
In the afternoon, another argument over the phone with B+. I called JL. We went to an Italian restaurant for dinner, and then to El Establo bar. Afterwards, I went alone to a brothel. I touched the breasts, very large but firm, natural, of a "sex worker," fat and funny, who had, in several places— face, shoulder, left breast—large moles like beans. I came home very late.

Midmorning, I call Tun to postpone our appointment until Monday. Embarrassment.

Friday.
No news from the chief. Reconciliation with B+, after three long phone conversations.
Reading Voltaire's *Memoir*.

Saturday.
Dinner with B+. I tell her about my idea of becoming a policeman.

She laughs at me. I insist that I'm serious.

"But you live outside the law," she tells me.

"That's why. I know the environment well," I answer.

"And you're going to walk around with a badge and uniform?"

"I would be a secret agent, what's wrong with you?"

B+ laughs again. We end up making a bet. If I become a police officer, she will grant me certain amorous favors that she has denied me until now.

"And where does the idea of becoming a policeman come from?" she asks me later.

"It could help me with what I am writing." And now I have an additional motivation: to win that bet.

"I do not think you will go to that extreme," she says.

I respond that she should not be so sure.

She changes the subject and reminds me that next week I have to go to Francisco Marroquín University, where she teaches grammar and literary composition classes, to give a talk to her students; she has required them to read some of my books.

In the afternoon we go to her parents' house on the Pacific coast.

Nighttime.

On the way to the coast, I told B+ that another of the reasons I was thinking of becoming a cop was that perhaps that way I could continue to research freely at La Isla, since I cannot do it at the Archive. And also, I added half-jokingly, so that I could contribute in a positive way to the fight against crime in the country.

"Do you want to become a national hero?" B+ laughed.

I answered, also laughing:

"Not quite. But we must broaden our perspectives. I think I would be a subversive policeman."

"I think that book, *Fouché*, is the one that has influenced you."

I told her that she was partly right.

We have just arrived at her parents' apartment, a luxury condominium facing the beach that is somewhat reminiscent of those enjoyed by wealthy Central Americans in Miami. But on this gray and muggy day the air conditioning and the elevator are appreciated: American comforts.

A little while ago B+ asked me to give her a massage. Her back, she said, hurt a lot. I am back to fantasizing about the idea of becoming a cop. But clearly just thinking about being part of the "forces of order" disgusts me.

Maybe the idea of becoming a policeman is less the influence of Fouché and more the result of a moral decline that has come, I think, from age rather than from study or experience. But where is the wisdom or self-knowledge that usually comes with age?

I had abandoned my Memoirs, *but many things that I found novel or fun made me go back to the absurdity of talking about myself with myself*, writes Voltaire toward the end of his book. *I'm almost ashamed to be happy watching the storms from the port.*

Guatemala City.

It's eleven at night. A very soft drizzle falls. I smoke some marijuana and listen to Ravel while I check my email. The phone rings. I get up. "Do not stir up the hornet's nest," someone says. Then click, the line goes dead.

Monday.

A recurring dream about Paul, who, although very old and sick, is still alive in Tangier. I want to go see him, but there are schedule conflicts. I am still a student (as in other recurring dreams, but these had never before been complicated with the topic of Paul alive again). I'm finishing my last year of school at Liceo Javier high school—which I did not complete—and I have final exams. Another complication: Pía, from whom I do not want to be away for too long, and I have already scheduled trips to Russia and Japan (which match my current plans in real life). I change plans, I decide to go to Tangier. I worry that Paul has not answered my latest letters, in which I ask him if he needs any money—the money generated by his book royalties. What if he were to answer yes, that he needs it? I wonder in the dream. Would I not have to pay him back the money I have received for those royalties and that I have already spent? But while I'm thinking about all this, and while I put on the school uniform—gray pants, white shirt, burgundy jacket—to go to school and take the exams, I realize that the reason I want to go to Tangier is that I would like to have Paul read what I am writing. I think it through: Paul is almost blind, he will not be able to read anything. But I can tell him what I'm doing, read bits of the text to him, see what he thinks. Suddenly, I have a volume of Paul's complete works in my hands. In it I find a series of articles and essays that I had not read, and of whose existence I was not aware. There is a very long one, about Alta Verapaz, and others about trips through Central America and tropical Africa, illustrated with color photographs. I am struck by one with the title "Music." Apparently, I translated it myself. I read the first sentence aloud: *Music is the most sonic organization of sounds*. A woman's voice (Alexandra?) asks: "Masonic?"

and laughs. She tells me the translation does not sound very good. I review the original English, and I confirm that the first sentence is much longer and more complex. I keep reading the essay, which consists of a series of definitions of the word "music" by famous composers and performers. There is something bombastic and convoluted in the phrasing of most of the definitions. Each one is accompanied by a picture of its author, but almost all them are wearing masks or costumes or wigs, which changes the text from pompous to comical.

I wake up thirsty. It is still nighttime. I get up to drink some water—I am thinking of a little house on Pasteur boulevard in Tangier, not too far from Paul's apartment, where perhaps I could stay if I manage to get back—and it is not until I turn on the light in the kitchen that I come to the realization that Paul died more than eight years ago. While the water flows from the faucet into a tin cup from Madras, I suddenly remember the moment when I kissed his already cold forehead in the Tangier morgue.

Tuesday.

Long interview with Benedicto Tun—which I have to interrupt (almost three hours into it) to go to the university and give a talk to B+'s students.

By way of introduction and as an apology for certain delays and postponed interviews in the past, Tun explains to me that his routine work currently consists of analyzing signatures and fingerprints in various kinds of documents, particularly for the Property Registry, Courts of Auditors, and several banks, since cases of fraud have proliferated dramatically in recent years.

He allows me to examine a copy of the ruling by his father in the case of a young French woman who participated in the kidnapping of Gordon Mein, the ambassador from the United States, in 1968. He shows me pictures of the young woman, who collaborated in the ambassador's kidnapping by renting in her own name the Avis car they used for the act. Then, when she found herself cornered by the police, she put a gun in her mouth and shot herself before they could arrest her.

He allows me to browse the copy of an undated letter (probably from the seventies) addressed to the president of the republic by residents of Zones 9 and 10. In it they mention that they have consulted with Tun, recently retired, requesting the improvement and modernization of the Bureau via the installation of an "IBM machine" to analyze the data from the thieves who operate in those residential areas. Neighbors propose that the financing of the machine will be "in the most disinterested way, for the improvement of the police service, as patriotic collaboration for the collective welfare."

An old man leaves the office next to Tun's and, seeing him go by, Benedicto gets up to call him. It is attorney Rodríguez. Benedicto introduces him to me and explains to him that I would like to ask him some questions. The old man says he's not in very good health but offers to grant me an interview a few days later, after he is done with the medical treatment he is currently receiving and that is causing him some discomfort.

I then ask Benedicto to tell me about the problem that his father had as a result of the ruling that he issued on the suicide of Mario Méndez Montenegro.

"It was during the government of Mario Mendez's brother, Julio César, when they arrested my father," he begins. "I myself went to get him out. But first I am going to tell you something that happened a few years earlier, because I think I did not do anything other than return a favor. I had friends on the left, which at that time was almost a crime, right? I never joined any subversive organization, although my friends tried to convince me, and I did attend some meetings, which were clandestine, of course.

"Returning from one of these one night, shortly after the 1963 coup, a friend and I were arrested. They took us in a jeep with official license plates to what was then the First Police Corps, where they had a place that you will remember, known as the Tiger's Den, where they kept political prisoners.

"One of the policemen interrogating us in a kind of office hit me in the face with a rubber club, the kind stuffed with steel pellets. The blow caused my nose to bleed. Instinctively, I defended myself; I snatched the club from the policeman's hand. Then, he asked his colleagues to help him get it back from me. But they didn't do it: 'He took it from you, *you* take it from him.' They wanted us to fight. I prepared myself, I raised the club, without thinking, of course. The cop, who did not want to risk getting hit, did not insist. He simply took out his gun and led my friend and me to the collective jail, the famous Tiger's Den. There, someone advised me to return the weapon to the policeman, because this little trick might later cost me. I listened to him, of course. And you know what? I remember that before tossing the club between the iron bars I saw the following inscription on the handle, in English, of course: 'Property of the United States Government,'" says Benedicto with a smile.

"There," he continues, "I met the brother of the famous 'Pepe' Lobo Dubón, Roberto, may he rest in peace, with whom I had a conversation for a good while. He died shortly thereafter, as you may know; he was shot by a soldier in a bar called Martita. He was very brave, no doubt about it. Anyway, we could see a young man they had just tortured,

142

his face disfigured and bruises everywhere, lying in a corner, possibly dying.

"Several hours later, a guard called out my name in a loud voice. Lobo Dubón warned me that if they took me out at that time of night, it was possible that they were thinking of killing me. He told me to be strong. I came out believing that everything ended there, but what happened was that someone had told my father that they had me in prison, and he came to get me out. Of course, I was not going to leave my friend there, so my father and I demanded his release. When they saw that they were letting us go, other prisoners asked us to appeal on their behalf on the grounds of unconstitutionality. They called out their names from the Tiger's Den, and I started to jot them down in the palm of my hand with a Parker pen that I had at the time and that I valued a lot because it was a gift from my father. But a policeman snatched it from me and snapped it in half."

Benedicto has to return a phone call that he received a few minutes ago on his cell phone. He excuses himself, and after talking for a while, he sits back down next to me on the white leatherette armchair. I ask him to tell me about his father's arrest.

"One afternoon," he begins, "in April of 1967, someone alerted me over the phone that my father was in custody. 'They have him in the First Corps barracks. They've already ordered prison food for him,' they told me, and I remember it very well because that was when I realized that it was serious. I spoke with several friends and acquaintances of my father and of the minister of the Interior at the time, asking for an explanation, but to no avail. In the upper spheres of politics, police, and the military, it would appear that they were unaware of the case. Then I decided to talk to a moneyed young man, who was influential in government. He owed me a couple of favors, and he agreed to give me a hand. He got me an interview with a high-ranking military official. Three men welcomed me into a 'dark house' (it was already nighttime by then) here, downtown. In these situations, you are received with all the lights off, so that you cannot see the faces of those who speak to you. I only managed to find out that it was a low-level matter, or a policy issue that had nothing to do with the government; otherwise the army would have known. I called Rodríguez then, and we decided to go directly to the barracks—not together, however, but one behind the other, so that they would not arrest the two of us at the same time. We synchronized our watches; it was almost eleven o'clock at night. I was able to go through the first door of the barracks without being stopped. I did not give them time to react, I suppose. In the parking lot I saw, in a fancy car, a relative of the president, who was leaving. I went up to the second floor, all the way to the Interpol department, at the end of the corridor, where there was light. They had my father there, under interrogation. He seemed disoriented, as if he had not yet realized that he was in custody. 'I'm working with these gentlemen,' he told me.

"They were reviewing his ruling on the suicide of Mario Méndez, the president's brother. They wanted my father to report that he had been assassinated. They wanted to make a hero out of him, a martyr.

"I told my father to get up, that I was there to take him with me. I grabbed him by the arm and pulled him out of there. When I got out to the hallway I heard Rodríguez arguing with one of the guards at the door. He was explaining to them that, in addition to being a lawyer, he was an army officer.

"When they let him through, he joined us and the three

of us went out to the street without any additional difficulties. On our way home, I told my father how they had alerted me that he was detained and that they had even ordered prison food for him. He did not want to believe it, but that very night we wrote his letter of resignation. The president, as I told you, did not accept it."

With some misgivings, I tell him that, in order to paint a clearer picture of his father, I would like to know some personal traits.

"Ah," he says, "my father's personality."

"Yes. For example, what books he liked to read. Judging from the way he wrote, I assume that he read quite a bit."

"It is true. He read everything." He smiles. "In addition to criminology, forensic medicine, and other sciences related to his work, he was interested in philosophy, the occult, and the esoteric—and in particular, palmistry."

Benedicto stops and studies the palm of his left hand for a while. With his right index finger, he touches, I believe, the wisdom line, which is very pronounced. "He believed . . . ," he says, and pauses. His mind seems to change course. "He also read history. He read a lot of Toynbee."

He shows me a photo from the sixties. In an austere amphitheater, Benedicto Senior is standing, in a formal suit, in front of a podium. He is delivering a talk at a Police Academy conference, his son explains to me. He has a strange grin and seems very tense, even tormented, and he has his arms crossed over his chest in a defensive attitude, the attitude typical of the very shy when facing the public.

"As you can see," the son tells me, "he was a very shy man. He was very quiet on the outside, but at home he spoke loudly and had an iron hand."

He tells me, not without signs of filial affection, that he

145

was the youngest of seven brothers and that he had only a few years with his father as an adult.

"He was internally conflicted about his Mayan origins," he tells me. "You know how things were. Things have changed, although in reality, maybe they have not have changed so much. Racial discrimination persists, right? Only now it is less crude than it was then."

He tells me that his father was the only son (he had three sisters) in a Quiché family from San Cristóbal Totonicapán. The father was a merchant and sent his son to high school at the county seat in Quezaltenango. Upon graduation, he traveled to the capital, where he started his law degree. Right after he began his studies, he found employment as a scribe for General José María Letona, a government minister and "right-hand man" for Manuel Estrada Cabrera [immortalized by Asturias as *el Señor Presidente*]. That job, which allowed him to familiarize himself with state matters (he had excellent handwriting, and the minister had him copy his own books), led to disagreements with his father, who did not want him to be a mere employee. He had made financial sacrifices to send him off to school in the capital with the hopes that he would pursue a college degree.

"My grandfather, who was mayor of his town for more than one term, had a store near that of the Gutiérrez family—can you imagine?" he continues. "If my father had devoted himself to business, perhaps he would have become a rich man, though perhaps not as rich as Juan Bautista Gutiérrez, from the Gutiérrez family in Totonicapán, one of the wealthiest families, if not *the* wealthiest, in Central America, right?" Benedicto smiles.

"The truth is that he continued his employment with the office of the president. He liked life in the capital, the

European suit and all that this city had to offer to a young college student, except for the little Panama hat that young dandies wore at that time. He never wore one. He did not want to return to San Cristóbal, so he continued as sub-secretary until the fall of Estrada Cabrera. As you know, his own minister, General Letona, testified about the mental incapacity of the dictator before the Legislative Assembly, who removed him from office. Then, my father had to flee to El Salvador. About a year later, he returned to Guatemala. After a brief time in jail, he was acquitted and began to work in what would later become the Identification Bureau.

"The Bureau," Benedicto continues, "completely consumed him; it was his sphere of power. He dedicated all his time to it, and conversely he tended to not take care of his family." He says this without a tone of complaint, stating it as simply another fact. He repeats that, outside the home, his father was very shy and reserved, but at home he could be very harsh.

"He asked everything of his children," says the youngest child, smiling, "but he did not give everything. To help support us, my mother had to take work as a seamstress. The salary from the Bureau was very low, as I already told you. But there he could innovate. He was a man with power, and his job was his refuge. As I mentioned, his Quiché Mayan origin was a problem for him. He also had mild speech problems, and that is why he did not like to speak in public."

I asked him if his father spoke Quiché.

"I believe that he did, as a child, but he forgot it. When we visited my grandmother at the village house, she and the other older ladies laughed at him and made jokes because he had forgotten his mother tongue. No one there used chairs or tables, everyone sat on a mat on the floor, but when we arrived they would take out tiny chairs, like toy chairs, where we could barely sit, and they set up a tiny table for us that would make you laugh," he tells me. "Imagine the things that he must have seen at work and that he had to keep quiet about," he continues. "Sometimes, at home, in his old age, he cried in silence. There were those who spoke ill of him, of course, because they were affected by his rulings or because they considered him part of the repressive machine, or because of prejudice, right? In any case, he did not cling to his position. He wanted to resign on more than one occasion, but his resignations were not accepted. Ydígoras Fuentes himself tried to remove him from office, and the chief of police opposed him."

I tell him that seems incredible.

"Did I already tell you about the corpse he had to go to identify one night, only there was no corpse?"

I say no, or that I do not remember.

"He told me about that when he was already very old, shortly after his retirement. The thing is, one night they took him and the Justice of the Peace, responsible for the removal of corpses, to a place on the outskirts of town, off the western highway. There were some policemen on the shoulder of the road, and they continued on foot to an area of open land. A police officer was there, next to a man lying on the ground among the bushes with a bullet wound in his back. The famous flight law, right? My father told me that he was sure that that he was a construction worker because of his attire. He leaned over to examine him, and he realized that he was not dead. 'There is no corpse here,' he said to the cops. 'This man is alive.' Then, the officer ordered one of the agents: 'Well, do your duty.' And the agent approached the man lying on the grass and shot him in the head," he tells me.

Afternoon.

After a very quick lunch and the talk at the university, I'm at the Hotel San Jorge with Javier Mejía, who called me a few days ago because he wanted to give me a copy of his last book, *The Foreign Agent*. Mejía was a cultural attaché in Washington and now he works for the Ministry of Foreign Affairs.

We talk about books (Ellison's *Invisible Man* comes up, as in almost all my conversations with this individual) and then, inevitably, about politics. I get very bored; rather than having a conversation, Mejía boasts or complains. As we are about to finish our coffees, Martín Solera—a criminal lawyer I met a few months earlier, at the workshop on policy and violence with Dr. Novales—appears. Solera asks me if I already received the diploma for attending the lecture series that he sent with Roberto Lemus, whom I suspect was a kidnapper. I say no. I explain that I had to suspend my visits to the Archive. The lawyer seems a little surprised. I assure him that it is nothing definitive; I have to talk to the chief and I hope that I will soon be able to revisit La Isla. It occurs to me to ask him for Lemus's phone number. I'm going to call him, I tell him, to see if he can give me the diploma, which, after all, I would like to have. I write down the number on a paper napkin.

After Solera leaves, when the coffees are paid for and we are about to say goodbye, Mejía tells me in a low voice that he knows the chief at the Archive Recovery Project very well.

"A very dark character. If they ever find a file on him, they will see how many ugly deaths have his name on them."

I make a face of hostile disbelief, and he continues:

"It is very ironic," he says, "that he would be the one who is sniffing around his enemies' Archives, no? He is himself a murderer."

Uncomfortable, wanting to change the subject, I mention

Fouché, and the anecdote told by Zweig about his end 'at peace with men and with God': with men, because shortly before his death he decided to burn the police files for which many powerful people feared him, and which he had taken with him when he left Paris, and with God, because he had time to confess and receive the lasts rites.

"I am not a Francophile," he comments scornfully. "The biography that I want to read is Kissinger's, but it is a seven-hundred-page tome and I have not had the time."

We say goodbye.

Of course (I think, once I am back in my car, as I watch the stocky author agent walk away with long strides, in his navy-blue suit, down Avenida Las Américas), in his current job, he inspires mistrust.

The chief has not called back.

Mechanically, with suppressed fear, thinking *I shouldn't*, I dial Lemus's number. No one answers.

Friday. Seven in the evening.

I meet with Mejía again, this time at a Mexican restaurant. (I wanted to ask him on what he based his reckless judgment of the chief.) I found a pretext for meeting: to give him one of my books, which he had told me he wanted to review. He arrives with a friend, a linguist and literary critic, who studied in Paris. *Bref*: a fop.

Mejía insists:

"Your chief is, or was, Comandante Paolo," he tells me, and laughs. "Didn't you know?"

I did not know, and I feel a little naive, a little dumb. What I did know is that "Comandante Paolo" was part of the court that sentenced the young guerrilla women captured in the eighties in Guatemala and later executed in Nicaragua; they were the ones that Dr. Novales referred to during his lecture series.

We argue about the definition of war crimes. Mejía compares the executions attributed to the chief with the crimes committed by the Guatemalan military. I do not see, I say, the symmetry.

I think Mejia's anger toward the chief at the Archive Recovery Project is of a personal nature. (As a young man, Mejía was an active member of the Guerrilla Army of the Poor, in which "Comandante Paolo" was a leader.) The amusing part is that Mejía now works for the government and finds it reprehensible that the chief is in charge of the Archive Recovery Project.

When we say goodbye, he surprises me by handing me an article that he is preparing, about the ensemble of all the books I have written. He would like to publish it, he tells me, in a foreign magazine. I read it when I get home. He surprises me again: the tone is slightly complimentary.

Monday, May 14.

I had lunch at my parents'. Long conversation with my father and Magalí. I ask them what they think we should do if we find out now who kidnapped my mother. My father says that he would do the same thing we have done so far: nothing.

"You know," I tell him, "kidnapping is an imprescriptible crime; it makes no difference if more than twenty years have gone by, there could still be punishment."

He does not change his mind.

When Magalí leaves, I ask my father if he has saved the

tapes we recorded during the phone negotiations at the time of my mother's kidnapping. He says he has. I ask him for them. He goes to one of his cabinets and finds three cassettes.

"You keep playing with fire," he tells me as he hands them to me.

Wednesday.

Yesterday morning, another interview with Benedicto Tun. He explains that he does not have much time; he must go to the courthouse to take care of some business. He tells me that his youngest son also wanted to be at this meeting but was not able to come because of work. I suggest that the three of us meet sometime in the future.

Among other criminal events that he remembers at random, he tells me about one known as "the case of house number 38." It was a robbery committed in the residence of two old women. They were killed by the robbers, among them the grandson of one of the women.

"At that time, you know, when the city was still very small, one investigation method in common use was to send agents to drink at the bars. Everyone knew everyone, and sooner or later you would hear something said by someone who was being careless that could serve as a clue. *One more down*, said the drunk each time he emptied a little bottle of firewater. That's why they arrested him and took him to the barracks, and it did not take long for him to talk. He was one of the culprits, and because of him, they found the other two."

Rodríguez appears. Benedicto introduces us again, and he accompanies us to the office next door before saying goodbye. Although Benedicto had already warned me that his friend suffers severe lapses of memory, I ask Rodríguez to tell me about Benedicto Senior. He says, "He was a brilliant man, honorable, extremely honest, deeply knowledgeable about his work. Our first criminologist. That is why they could not do without him, not even during the Revolutionary Government. He was a close friend of intellectuals like Balsells Rivera, the writer, and Cazali, the father of that girl who writes art reviews in the press. . . . He came from Quiché; his parents were Indian people. And look how far he got."

I ask him to tell me about the failed uprising against the regime of Ydígoras Fuentes in 1960, in which he played a significant role. His memory, however, is too fuzzy and he cannot string together the events. About Yon Sosa (who also participated in the uprising and was the founder of the Armed Rebel Forces), he tells me: "It's a pity that he would come to such an end. They killed him last year in Tapachula for smuggling; didn't you hear about it?"

I know that members of the Guatemalan army killed him in Tapachula, but that was more than forty years ago. I choose to remain silent.

Sunday, May 26.
Pía turns five. Small celebration with my parents and sisters in El Tular. Penguin mini-piñata, that at the moment of truth Pía refuses to break.

Monday.
Silent call last night, around two. Pía was with me, which worries me even more.

Tuesday.
In the afternoon I went to Novex, the hardware store, looking for a nylon rope and harnesses for a possible escape (with Pía) through a window of the apartment. At the end the

idea seemed ridiculous to me and instead I bought cables and terminals to record phone conversations.

Monday.

Good times with Pía, who is on vacation. At night I'll take her to her mother's.

In the morning, a call (that I let the answering machine take) from Uli Stelzner—"the German documentarian," as he describes himself in the message he leaves. He is the director of the film *Testament*, about the life of Alfonso Bauer Paiz, a political activist and survivor of more than one murder attempt, and still active at almost ninety—a splendid and rare example of a good Guatemalan leftist from the twentieth century. Someone told Uli that I have been working at the Archive. He wants us to talk; he invites me to have coffee with him one of these days. I call him back in the afternoon. I ask who told him that I had been visiting the Archive. "Some people," he responds. I tell him that this week I will be very busy; we agree to talk next week.

"Some people." Why not a straight answer? I wonder.

At night.

"To love someone who does not love you," says B+, who has just read *One Hundred More Poems from the Japanese* by Kenneth Rexroth, which I lent her a few days ago, "is like entering a temple and worshipping the wooden butt of a hungry idol."

"I think I understand. Whose is that?" I ask her.

"My own."

"I do not believe you."

"It doesn't surprise me. I don't care," she responds with some bitterness.

Wednesday.

I pick Pía up at school. I speak with her teacher. On Friday I will read an adaptation of a Quiché myth about the origin of corn to her class, a story about a crow and a woodpecker that show mankind the way to Paxil Hill, where the plant grew naturally.

The teacher continues to tell me about something that she started to share with me a few days ago. Yesterday, she says, she witnessed a homicide in front of her house. It was not her, after all, that those two men were watching! She is very frightened.

She also tells me that a few years ago she lived in Mexico, where she met a former Guatemalan guerrilla woman, who had been tortured by the police. She survived, and now leads a "normal life" in London. This woman told her that, over time, she came to forgive her torturers, but not her former bosses. One day, the war already over, she went to see Gaspar Ilom, the *comandante* (Rodrigo Asturias, Miguel Ángel's son), to tell him what she thought of him: that he was a pig. "He, Gaspar Ilom," the teacher says, "turned green, but he did not say anything."

Friday.

Last night I went with Magalí to the old post office to watch a documentary about the children of the guerrilla fighters, titled *The Hive*, which focuses on children of high- and middle-level teams in the Guerrilla Army of the Poor. Uli, the German documentarian, was there. He approached me to ask me what I thought of the film. The documentary is monotonous, but it is not without interesting moments. I said: "It's a family portrait, right? What can you expect?"

Uli made a slightly more severe criticism. "He [the director of the documentary is the son of an ex-*comandante* and was raised in a 'hive'] should not have done it, that boy was one of those children. Impossible to be objective."

We talked about one of the cases that the film presents: a woman, about twenty-five years old, who at the age of about ten got the news that her father had died in combat. A few years later someone told her that, in reality, her father had been accused of treason, tried by a guerrilla tribunal, and executed by his own comrades-in-arms. (When narrating this, the woman starts sobbing.) Somewhat later, she revealed that she heard another version: friends told her that her father had been a hero, that he did not commit treason, that that had been a mistake, a confusion. "I've always remembered my father," the interviewee says at the end, "as someone who fought for his homeland."

Uli, I believe rightly, complained that they did not probe deeper into this case. Who judged the supposed traitor? What was he accused of? What was the mistake, if there was one? "The fighters knew," I told him, "that if they were captured, death awaited them, or, if they were very lucky, exile—right?" (Death by their captors, or by their former comrades, because the danger of denunciations under torture or the monitoring of prisoners upon their release was widespread.)

"Of course," Uli agreed, and continued in a confidential tone, with his marked German accent: "I want to make a documentary about La Isla, but about the people who work there, at the Archive. That is why I wanted to talk to you. I know many of them. They are mostly former guerrillas or sons of former guerrillas. It's strange that someone like you was allowed to go in."

"You see," I said, "they can make exceptions. Anyway, it is good that those who took up arms to fight the system that has been left partly reflected there, at the Archive, continue to oppose it, let's say, legally, in a way that is retrospective and nonviolent—right?"

Luis Galíndez, from the Archive, came up to greet us. As always, he was very kind. He asked me why I have not returned to La Isla. I mentioned the complaints from other archivists over the privilege that I had been granted. He asked me (to my surprise) who gave me that news. I told him it was the chief.

"I see," he replied, "they sugarcoated it for you."

"And what would it be without the sugar?" I asked him in a joking tone.

"A tad more bitter," he said.

Uli, who seems to be aware of my case, commented:

"Of course, those decisions are made at the very top."

"I suppose that is the same top where they decided to give me the privilege to enter," I told him. "They decided to give me the privilege, and then to take it away from me. Seems right to me."

"Oh, well, how democratic," Galíndez said. "But it's true, they did you a favor by letting you in. And perhaps also when they did not let you come back," he laughed. Uli and I laughed with him.

"Anyway," Uli continued, "everybody should have access to these documents."

"Actually," I said, "I think there's nothing that we do not already know. A lot of details, nothing else." (But, I ask myself, isn't that how the old saying goes: that it is precisely in the details where God is—*lurking*?)

Midmorning, I dial Lemus's number. I think I recognize his voice from the answering machine. It sounds like it does on the cassettes. I hang up, quite scared. I redial and this time I record the voice. Then I call Benedicto Tun. He does not answer.

Shortly before noon, I go to Pía's school to read the adaptation of the Quiché myth about corn. In the afternoon, exhausted.

Sunday.

Last night the doorbell rang around midnight, while I was sleeping. This is it. They're coming for me. Another ring finished the job of waking me up. With a leap, I got up, confused, thinking about the rope and the harnesses that I had not bought to go out the window and lower myself down into the ravine. I said to myself: Pía isn't here, it doesn't matter. I left my room, filled with fear, and went through the darkness to the front door. "Who is it?" I asked. "Me," said B+ (early in the evening we had quarreled—as usual, absurdly). I turned on the light, I opened the door.

"Are you drunk?" I asked her. "What's wrong? You scared me."

She explained with a smile, half naughty, half guilty, that she wanted to be with me. I think that she does not imagine, cannot imagine, how much she frightened me.

"How many times did you ring the bell? I asked.

"Twice."

"I thought so."

I returned to bed with her, my heart still pounding.

Monday.

I ask myself if, after all, I really love B+. I answer my own question: yes.

After lunch at my parents'.

While we were eating, my father told me that this weekend he saw a television report about the Archive. Then we talked about the movie *Capote*. My father attacked the writer. "A real self-absorbed son of a bitch," he said. María Marta and I defended him, with the argument that Capote's friendly behavior (although self-serving) toward the unfortunate and terrible Perry Smith must have provided the latter, after all, some consolation.

"Let's see if the same thing that happened to Capote doesn't happen to you, and on account of researching criminals you never finish another book," said my father toward the end of the conversation.

Earlier this morning, the urologist definitively forbade my mother coffee and salt. A sad day, no doubt. At night, the sound of the rain, the quiet company of books.

Tuesday.
Pía has been sleeping peacefully for two hours. I wonder if I have actually played with fire by wanting to write about the Archive. It would have been much better if a former fighter, or a group of ex-fighters, and not a mere dilettante (with a very marginal perspective) were to be the first to expose to light what can still be exposed to light and remains hidden in that magnificent labyrinth of papers. As a discovery, as a Document or Testimony, the importance of the Archive is undeniable (although unbelievable, and unfortunately there are those who would like to deny it), and if I have not been able to make it a novel, as I thought I could, it's because I have lacked luck and fortitude.

Wednesday morning.
I call Tun's office several times; nothing. I wonder if he

can see my number when I call him, and he has decided not to answer. Or if he is sick, or on vacation. I'll call him again tomorrow.

I read an opinion by Voltaire about the grandson of Henry IV, Duke of Vendôme, which I would like to see applied to me: "Intrepid like his grandfather, a kind, giving character, who knew no hate, no envy, and no revenge. By dint of hating pomp, he came to a cynical carelessness that is unprecedented."

Friday.
Yesterday I called Tun again. He told me that he was in Mazatenango for several days, working, that he wanted to call me but had not had time. We agreed on lunch next Tuesday at La Casa de Cervantes, which is close to his office. I told him I had a favor to ask. Could he do a voice analysis? I need to compare, I told him, voices in some recordings. He said yes.

Saturday, June 8.
Day practically lost, with family.

Sunday.
In El Tular. Rain.

What can be thought must surely be fiction—Savater?

Monday.
Clara could not come to clean the apartment. She called me on the phone to explain that yesterday they killed another driver on the Boca del Monte bus line, where she lives, and today his fellow drivers are on strike.

Afternoon.

I call the chief at noon. To my surprise, he answers. The tone is very friendly. He apologizes to me for the string of missed appointments. He tells me that now he is more relaxed. The Human Rights Ombudsman has been reelected and the Project is not in danger, at least not for the duration of the next term, which lasts four years. And the San Antonio sinkhole is no longer a serious threat; they have everything ready in case an emergency evacuation is necessary. He asks me how "the book project" is going. I tell him I'm not sure, that I've been keeping a journal, and I don't know what I will do with it. "A journal?" he asks. I explain to him that it is a personal journal, where I use my visits to the Archive as a theme, and since the day of my suspension it has a *leitmotif*: my multiple calls to him that are never returned. He laughs and apologizes again. I have a confidential conflict, I say to him, and there is something I need to discuss with him. It is a rumor I have heard, a story that concerns him. I have recorded it as such in my journals, but I do not know if I should publish it, should the opportunity arise. On the other end of the line, I hear him cough. He suggests that we see each other immediately. We agree to meet for lunch at La Estancia.

He arrives ten minutes late. From one end of the long main room of the steak house, I watch him approach; he has a slight swagger as he walks, the way tall men often do. There is something of a Jesse James about him, with his faded jeans and checkered shirt. He has a poker player's gaze, underscored by large, dark, permanent circles under his eyes. I rise to greet him.

While we eat I tell him what Mejía has told me about the execution of people from his own ranks, attributed to him.

"That's true," he tells me, "and it's no secret."

He himself made statements before the Commission for Historical Clarification immediately after the signing of the Peace Agreements, and he relates that episode, which he characterizes as an error. When he testified, he adds, he asked that his civil name appear on the testimonial, but it was a guiding principle of the Commission not to use real names under any circumstances.

"But there is something that is not accurate in those rumors. I was a founder of the Guerrilla Army of the Poor. I was always part of a political cadre, I never had a military rank. I did not fight with weapons. The army—the enemy," he clarifies, "gave me the title of commander, I guess to make me seem important." I ask him if it would bother him if I publish the story. He shakes his head and adds that I can use his real name.

"There's something I want to clarify," he tells me, "about those executions. I am also referring to the executions mentioned in the documentary you saw with Uli and Galíndez. I lay claim to my role as a revolutionary, but I also like to recognize my mistakes. I had to explain what happened to several children of the comrades that we had executed, rightly or wrongly, because we were wrong more than once. Some leaders would have preferred that they not be told anything, that they continue to think that their parents had died or disappeared in action. That did not seem right to me, but when I complained, they told me that, if I wanted, I could myself explain what happened. That's what I did, no matter how much it cost me. You do not, cannot, know how much it cost me."

He remains silent for a moment and then continues; now his voice is somewhat more serious.

"Talking about it, everything seems a bit light, but this is something very serious. It is probably what worries me the most at this point in life. It is, not in a figurative sense but in a literal sense, a matter of life and death for me. I was fighting to the death then. I think I'm the only jerk who still thinks about all this."

He pauses again, and I seem to detect a hint of moisture in the whites of his eyes that I had not seen before.

"Those executions within our ranks, I recognize that they were errors, or exaggerations, excesses of severity, when they were not atrocities. Admitting this has not been easy, and what bothers me now is not having been more strongly opposed to the application of those drastic measures, which I was not in agreement with in many cases. If I could go back. . . . But that was another time." The features of his face, which are rather hard, have now softened a bit. "There are those who, even knowing that we executed their relatives, have not lost their revolutionary spirit. And it's strange, but, on the other hand, there are also many who would have preferred never to know the truth."

He tells me of a particular case, the murder of a journalist for which the State has taken responsibility. Despite the fact that, according to what he knows to be true, this woman was executed by order of the leaders of the guerrilla organization to which she belonged, her own relatives prefer to ignore this because there is the possibility of collecting compensation from the State, which would be impossible if the murder were attributed to the guerrillas.

"I would like to talk to you about all of this when we have more time," he says, insisting on the vital importance to him of these struggles of conscience.

I tell him that I am to go on a trip very soon (I do not tell him where, and he does not ask). I promise to give him, on my return, a draft of the text that I am writing about the Archive. I assure him that I will not make it public without his consent.

Finally, in a humorous tone, he tells me that he has had labor problems with a group of young researchers at the Archive. A local newscast aired an item yesterday, without disclosing its sources, about how he and others in positions of responsibility at the Project are accused of mistreating their employees. "This job is worse than managing a factory," the former guerrilla leader says with a smile.

We split the bill down the middle.

Tuesday.

On the way downtown, I call Benedicto on my cell phone to confirm our lunch date at La Casa de Cervantes. He has to cancel: he has been called at the last minute by a client who is waiting for him at the courthouse. He wanted to call me earlier, but he couldn't find my number. We can, if I agree, have lunch next Thursday, same place. Instead of continuing on downtown I turn around and go to Zone 14, for lunch at my parents'.

Thursday.

Meeting with Benedicto Tun and his son Edgar at the agreed-upon place. Mediocre lunch, cordial conversation. Before his son arrives, I give Benedicto two audiocassettes: one with the voice of Lemus that I recorded from his answering machine message, and the other with a short fragment copied from cassettes recorded during negotiations over my mother's kidnapping. He says that he should be able to share the results with me within two or three days.

He tells me another family anecdote, about the kidnapping by guerrillas and subsequent police arrest of one of his brothers, a pediatrician, in 1970.

About the Tun family, he says later, someone once said in public, while his father was still alive, "It is like a rosebush. It has roses, but also thorns." He explains that "thorns" probably referred to him, because of his left-wing ideas.

His son arrives. He wanted to meet me because he has read some of my books, he says. He writes plays. I see a clear resemblance to his grandfather, based on the photo that Benedicto (who, by the way, does not look like either of them) showed me.

Edgar Tun is a young man, about twenty-five, thin, frail-looking, and bright. He brings his own lunch, seasoning it with virgin olive oil, which he also brings with him. He suffers from a pancreas ailment, he explains. He studied legal and social sciences, and he now works as a researcher in the Reparation Program for Victims of the Armed Conflict.

Benedicto talks about the death of Turcios Lima, generally attributed to a traffic accident in Calzada Roosevelt of Guatemala City. According to Benedicto's father, who photographed the remains of the car in which the guerrilla leader traveled with his girlfriend and his mother, it was an attack. "The car, a Mini Cooper, caught fire too fast," says the son. "They may have used white phosphorus, but the cause of the fire, according to my father, could not have been just gasoline. In any case, it was said that if it was an attack it would have been by the Guatemalan Workers' Party, who had decided to eliminate Lima for lack of discipline."

He, Benedicto the son, met Turcios Lima as a teenager. Lima was the younger of the two, and very restless, Benedicto says. He was the godson of the archbishop of Guatemala,

Monsignor Casariegos, and, as I understand it, the archbishop's home was once the scene of his love affairs.

Benedicto also shares some details about the murder of the German ambassador, Karl von Spretti, in 1970. Not all members of the Rebel Armed Forces group that kidnapped him wanted to execute him when the government refused to release the political prisoners that were part of the negotiation. "They almost started shooting at each other," he tells me, "because they could not come to an agreement." This is something that was told to him by a friend of his who belonged to that group, and who later disappeared. He was among those who opposed the execution. "Upon getting the news that he had been captured, his girlfriend called me. I went to her house, and she showed me, among other things, letters that Von Spretti had written during his abduction. She kept them hidden behind a mirror. I read them, and then we burned them. Saving something like that in those days was too compromising."

He also talks about a Swiss journalist who visited Guatemala in the time of Ubico. Accused of being a communist, he was executed by firing squad at the penitentiary in the capital. While in prison, he had become friends with Benedicto's father, who did not think he was guilty. Before being executed, the Swiss man gave him a portable typewriter, which Benedicto's son still has today.

At noon, on a cloudy day, with the smell of rain, in the silver Lexus, between traffic lights, I think about my weaknesses. I have a light sense of remorse, and as a result, the thought that perhaps one has to be a bit immoral to be a moral person, at least in certain aspects, in order to understand the "mechanism" of morality.

Friday.

Long interview with Uli at Taco Bell. He's still thinking of making a documentary about La Isla. The mother of his "partner" who works at the Archive, he tells me, was captured by agents of the National Police many years ago and was never seen again. They are still seeking her whereabouts. It seems that, among the documents at the Archive, there is something about her capture. As a result of this, Uli visited the general cemetery in La Verbena. In the entry books, he tells me, there is data of great interest "if one is looking for the disappeared," with details about the origin and general features of the corpses. I speak to him extensively about Benedicto Tun.

Sunday. Father's Day.

In the afternoon, after a strange and pleasant day, but with a bitter end, B+ tells me by phone that she does not want to see me tomorrow, or for a few days—that she needs "time to think."

Monday.

In the morning I call Tun. He had the tapes analyzed, he tells me, and he believes that it is the same voice. "It is not irrefutable proof, mainly because the samples are not from the same period, right? But it is pretty certain."

I think of Lemus: pathetic, somber. This was, then, the Minotaur that awaited me at the center of the labyrinth in the Archive. From such a labyrinth, such a Minotaur. He is probably as scared of me as I am of him. If I attacked him, I wonder, would he defend himself?

Almost midnight. Two calls, one immediately after the other.

At the other end of the line, silence, maybe the sound of rain, but it is not raining tonight in Guatemala City.

Tuesday.

Until today I had not seriously thought about stopping the writing of this journal, but it is as if the germ of the end has already contaminated the organism.

I got an email from Guillermo Escalón, who has just returned from Paris. I call him on the phone and we agree to have dinner tomorrow.

Long-distance call from Homero Jaramillo. He needs to check some information—the phone number and the exact address of my apartment (where he lived for most of 2003). He is filling out forms to request an extension of his asylum in Canada, he explains. Jovial tone, as almost always. When I hang up, I have a sinking feeling.

The most precious thing in life is uncertainty—Kenko.

Thursday.

Last night I had dinner with Guillermo, after accompanying my father and Magalí to hospitalize my mother. They have inserted a catheter to drain the urine and prevent her defective kidney from collapsing. Long talk with Guillermo about the project at the Archive. Uli has invited Guillermo to work with him on the documentary that he is making. Guillermo has not given a final answer. I told him that the idea of a documentary in the making makes me want to stop writing about the Archive, that the cameras will do a better job than me.

Friday.

Call from Uli. He leaves for Germany on Sunday. He

wants to let me watch a documentary filmed by the Human Rights Ombudsman on the discovery of the Archive. We will not be able to see each other before his departure, but he will leave a copy for me at the house of a friend of his.

Monday, nighttime. Hotel Caimán.

On the Pacific coast with Pía, who is on vacation.

I was trying to sort these notes, this collection of notebooks, when she, who had been insisting for several minutes that I tell her a story, asked me what I was doing. I told her that I was trying to put together a story.

"For children?" she asks me.

I say no.

"For grown-ups?"

I tell her that I do not know, that maybe it's just for me.

"You know how it could end?" she tells me.

I shake my head.

"With me crying, because I can't find my dad anywhere." I laugh, surprised. Where did that come from? I ask myself. I listen for a while to the endless rumble of the great ocean waves.

Author's Note

More than ten years ago, when I visited the place known as La Isla for the first time—where the Historical Archive of the Guatemala National Police is currently housed—rescuing that sordid accumulation of papers and aberrations was still an ambitious and risky project, which on more than one occasion came close to being cancelled. Today the Archive is public (http://archivohistoricopn.org); the painstaking work of cataloging millions of police documents has facilitated the legal clarification of cases regarding the disappearance of persons and other crimes against humanity.

I want to thank Gustavo Meoño, Director of the Archive Recovery Project, who allowed me, a fiction writer, to venture onto that island.

Rodrigo Rey Rosa
2017

Postscript

The Guatemalan National Police Archive (AHPN) has become a world reference. Nearly 24 million folios of documents have been processed and their digital images are available for public consultation inside and outside of Guatemala. Hundreds of relatives of missing persons, who for decades have sought in vain to know something about the whereabouts of their loved ones, have requested and obtained valuable information from the Archive. The prosecutors who are in charge of investigating the atrocities committed during the years of the Guatemalan internal war have found in this Archive information and documentary evidence to contribute to more than a dozen trials. The judges have given them evidentiary value and these documents have contributed to sustaining harsh sentences against high-ranking military and police chiefs.

However, in August 2018 something unexpected happened. Just after one of the most consequential trials—due to the high status of the condemned generals—the government of Guatemala decided to intervene in the Archive. The director, Gustavo Meoño, was dismissed after thirteen years of work. A third of the qualified personnel were also dismissed as of December of this year, and the rest of the workers are in a state of total uncertainty about what will happen in the future. Multiple highly respected voices have spoken in solidarity with the Archive in more than twenty countries. There are many clouds that hover over this valuable documentary collection; the dangers that lie in wait for it are great indeed.

December 2018

Translator's Acknowledgments

I would like to thank Kristin Siracusa Fisher for her invaluable insights and recommendations as first reader of this English version; Marian Schwartz and AATIA's Literary Special Interest Group (LitSIG) for their input workshopping early excerpts from this translation with me; and Inés ter Horst, Angelica Lopez-Torres, and Lynne Chapman of the University of Texas Press for their kindness and support. I am also grateful to Rodrigo Rey Rosa for trusting me with his work and the good conversations about words.

Eduardo Aparicio
2018